Catching Moonlight

Catching Moonlight

EMILY MAH

Published by WorkHorse Productions, Inc.

Edited by Trent Zelazny.

Cover & Interior designed and formatted by:

www.emtippettsbookdesigns.com

To my sister-in-law, Tianne, her husband Jeff,
and kids Carsyn, Ty, Elly and Kinsley.
Here's hoping for no more collapsing garage ceilings or muskrat
invasions! (These two events were not directly related.)

ONE

"We wanted to know how you fare, Corban Alexander," said the genderless voice of the tribunal.

They had me sitting interrogation style. A light shone in my face so that I couldn't see who spoke. As if it wasn't any of my business who sat in judgment over me.

Don't snap at them, said the little voice of conscience in my head. My nerves were raw and had been for years. Gone was the time when a decade could pass in the blink of an eye. Now every day was long, and slow, and difficult. I was always on the verge of losing my temper.

"Well, I'm still here, aren't I?" I said. *I showed up when you summoned me*, I added in my mind. At least it was peaceful in the Citadel. No humans for at least a mile, which meant no human emotion in the air.

Up until yesterday, I'd been working in a refugee field hospital in Northern Africa. That place had enough pain and anguish and frustration and fear roiling through it to choke a being like me. Or it should have. The truth was, I could have gobbled it all and still been hungry for more.

"Be honest," the tribunal demanded, as if reading my thoughts.

"I'll keep fighting the good fight, but as I've asked before: Are you sure there's no procedure to deal with the likes of me? You really wanna wait until I lose control before you hunt me down?"

"That is not funny."

I wasn't joking. I'd ascended two thousand years ago, after a brief mortal life as a Roman citizen. I'd seen when a coterie of angels broke their vows, fell, and took Rome and much of its empire down with them. The battles had seared themselves into my memory, and the most dangerous fallen angels had been the oldest ones. Now, I was older than any member of that coterie had been. I was a ticking time bomb. There was a time when the angelic order's forgiving nature comforted me. Now it scared me spitless.

And I hated sitting still. I hated feeling exposed under the light. I wanted to run, to climb, to get away from all scrutiny.

"Must you always be a pessimist?" chided the tribunal.

Yes. The consequences of pride were dangerous for supernaturals like me. After the fall of Rome, I'd thrown myself into my work completely, honoring my covenants, serving and protecting humanity, and keeping humans at arm's length—they were never friends, and certainly never anything more. Until…

"Did you summon me to talk about Liana?" I asked. "Is she safe? Did something happen?"

Her name put a stab of grief through my heart. I'd met her when she was eighteen. She would be twenty-two now. She'd been infected with vampirism, yet somehow managed what no one else in human history ever had: to fight it and retain her human soul. Every morning she would face sunrise to burn the vampiric taint out of her body. Few could withstand that pain, and any normal vampire would die trying such a stunt.

And even with vampirism in her system, she could see me. She always saw me, no matter how I'd drawn my supernatural veil around myself.

I'd done my best to help her along. My healing touches also helped keep the vampirism at bay, and when she'd turned fully vampire in order to access her supernatural powers and kill her grandsire, I'd healed her in the ultimate, most intimate way possible for an angel. I'd kissed her, letting har vampirism burn me to the core so that I lost my powers for a full year and blasted the evil taint out of her for good.

It hadn't been an entirely selfless act, though. While I had been able to ignore pretty faces and hourglass bodies at my age, I hadn't been able to ignore someone who fought so hard against such long odds. When she began to look at me not as an angel, but as a man, my heart had been hers. Even so, I'd had no idea what a big mistake that kiss would be.

Now, my fall was inevitable; I ached to push the boundaries, break all my vows, and let go. I spent every day putting it off another hour, another minute, any amount of time I could buy with faith and sacrifice.

The tribunal sighed. "Melanie has discovered that her sister, Darissa, is dead."

My silent, stoney heart sank.

Darissa, whom Liana had killed, had been one of three powerful vampire sisters who loved each other with the kind of love only family and long association could foster. Born over two millennia ago in the Nabatean Empire, they were some of the strongest, wiliest vamps in all of history.

The oldest sister, Gamlat, had disappeared a few hundred years ago and was likely dead. We couldn't say for sure. She had rarely strayed far from her original home, even though her civilization was now ruins in modern-day Jordan. She'd also kept her Nabatean name, even during her long stints in New England to spend time with her sisters. The second sister, who went by Melanie nowadays, had become a hermit around the time Gamlat had disappeared. Whenever we found her, she seemed to be doing arcane research that we weren't equipped to analyze.

Especially not after all of the damage the order had suffered at the hands of Darissa, the youngest.

She'd been the bane of our existence. Her relentless, twenty-five hundred year campaign had almost destroyed us dozens of times. Her attacks had hollowed us out as she exterminated all of our scholars and archivists. All of the support roles that allowed us to remember our history and secrets of who and what we were now stood empty. She'd also nearly destroyed our archives and the Citadel itself. None of our warriors had been able to prevail against her, but little, mortal Liana had caught her off guard and ended the nightmare.

My being ached at that memory too. How could I get over someone like her? I didn't even want to try. When someone like that looked twice at you, you didn't look away.

We'd known that hiding Darissa's death from Melanie wouldn't be possible, long term, but I had hoped we could manage it for a few more years, or even decades. Apparently the jig was up.

"So Liana is in danger," I said.

"Yes, Liana is in danger."

"But… she lives?" I tried to hide the curiosity that burned like a beacon in me.

"She does. Her vampirism is also returning, though. Slowly, but unmistakably."

What? I'd thought I had cured her vampirism with my kiss. I hadn't even managed that? I slouched in my seat. "Is she well?" I asked. "Is she happy?"

"Why don't you ask her yourself?"

It took me a moment to absorb that. Once I did, though, I shot to my feet, hands balled into fists. "No." I wanted to see her more than anything, and that was the problem. Besides, she'd suffered enough in her life. She didn't need an unstable immortal in the mix.

"Corban…"

"No. Send someone else. You are a *fool* if you send me to her. An *idiot*."

"I can't send anyone else. The council has ruled against extending her protection, but you, I know, will say that's wrong."

The council was the legislature of sorts that ruled the angelic order. Lately, they'd made some questionable decisions. "I promised Liana the order would look out for her," I said. "She has a human soul. We can't abandon her."

"Yes, yes, I know your feelings on this. That is why I'm offering you the chance to go to her. To be clear, it's the only chance she has for angelic protection."

Did my protection even count as "angelic?" I was an angel, but my feelings for her... "You're offering this against the wishes of the council?"

"That is the right of the inner circle. We, who hold the secrets of what it means to be ascended, sometimes see things that the rest of you do not."

"Then you go protect her. Or send someone else from the inner circle." The higher level politics of the order gave me a headache. The 'inner circle' was a shadowy organization that operated on its own, able to do what it wanted no matter what the council said. I wanted nothing to do with them, despite their repeated invitations that I join.

"It is you or no one."

"But it can't be me!"

"Why not? You promised her you would see her again."

"Th-that... that was a private conversation..." The words came out weak. The order had a right to listen in on my phone calls. I shouldn't have made that promise. It was another sign that I wasn't fit to serve anymore.

"Well, now you can keep your promise," said the tribunal.

"I love her," I confessed. "I'm weak around her. That's why I need to stay away from her. She's only a girl—a child compared to me."

"Yes, well… You won't be anything more than her protector. And as I've said, old friend, it is you or no one. You are being offered this chance once and only once. Decide."

Going to her was a fool's errand, and my kind was supposed to fear to tread where fools rushed in. This moment was a test, like Eve being offered the apple. If I made the wrong choice, the consequences could be catastrophic for the world.

And yet, I'd already made the choice. All I was struggling with was whether or not to voice it. "Send me to her," I said.

THREE HOURS LATER I was on a plane tearing through the sky to Newark, New Jersey. I and the other passengers were packed like sardines into a noisy metal tube, the air awash with mild anxiety and anticipation that did not even begin to sate my hunger.

Since I couldn't sit still, I stalked the aisles. My kind had what we referred to as a "veil," an ability similar to invisibility that made people either not see us, or if they saw us, not take note of us or remember much about us. I hadn't realized how powerful it was until it was gone for the year after I kissed Liana.

One toddler saw me as I took in her frilly little dress, perfectly stitched and embroidered in rich purple, a dye that had been so rare in Roman times that only royalty wore it. People had *so much* clothing these days, so many outfits. Her blue eyes fixed on me every time I walked past. I gave her what I hoped was a beneficent smile—things that had once been second nature to me were now a struggle.

Little voices at the back of my mind taunted me. This miraculous flying contraption was flimsy enough that if I stormed the cockpit and sent it into a dive, delicious fear would explode from all these helpless passengers. If I stabbed someone and produced a gushing wound, delectable screams would fill the air. I wanted to be awash in human pain and guzzle it down until my whole being buzzed with power. This was my normal these days.

I could feel the sheath of my dagger strapped to my forearm every time I flexed my muscles. I skimmed off everyone's anxiety even though it was like licking up raindrops while I was parched and famished.

Liana needed help, but she was getting me instead. What would she think of what I'd become? I wasn't the benevolent angel-boy I'd been when we'd last met.

I hadn't been for years.

TWO

I arrived on campus in the mid-morning. Princeton had already been abandoned by most of the students. Those who remained to pack up their masses of belongings were nervous, but not nervous enough to make the air shimmer even a little bit. I climbed out of my Uber and into the sweltering humidity. Some groundskeepers were mowing the lawns and I could smell the fresh cut, sun-baked greenery. Being back in the US meant being even more in the world of machines; Northern Africa had cars and tractors and such, but here it was as if half the population was mechanical or computerized or both. It was so far beyond what I thought I'd ever live to see, and so far beyond what I could have explained to my long dead family.

None of the gardeners looked up as I climbed the stairs to Liana's dorm. They probably didn't even see me.

Inside, the hallways were quiet. I ghosted along, checking the door numbers until I found hers. The sound of someone coughing in the distance echoed off the tile floors and through the empty rooms. I took a deep breath before knocking.

A girl with deep olive skin, dark hair, and copious amounts of silver and turquoise jewelry opened the door. I took a step back. This wasn't Liana, but rather Gina Rodriguez, one of Liana's friends from Taos High. She couldn't see me, and was looking up and down the hall with a bemused frown, no doubt wondering why she'd opened the door.

Behind her was a girl with even darker skin and hair, and much less jewelry: Amy Blackhawk, Liana's other close friend from high school. She craned her neck to see what Gina was doing, but soon turned back to stuffing clothes into a plastic bin.

"Who is it?" asked a way too familiar voice.

Her voice. Liana's.

"No one," said Gina. "I think I'm just hearing things." She moved to close the door.

But a pale hand stopped her and pulled the door open wider. A young woman leaned around to see who it was. As always, my veil did not work on her. At the sight of me, she froze.

So did I. My memories of how she looked had faded in the last four years. Seeing her face brought them back with a vengeance. She hadn't aged much, but who does in four years? Her brown hair was about waist length and her dark eyes were the same deep pools I'd risked getting lost in countless times. Her skin was porcelain pale and she and her two friends could have been on a tourism poster advertising the three cultures of New Mexico: Anglo (Liana), Hispanic (Gina), and Native (Amy.)

Slowly she stood up straight and stepped all the way into view. "Corban," she said, with an uneasy glance at Gina.

That always lifted my veil for others, when a person talked to me in plain view like this.

Gina blinked. "Oh, hi."

"Hey, Corban," said Amy, looking up.

Their minds would have manufactured a narrative to make my sudden appearance make sense. I'd just walked up, or they'd overlooked me before. These two knew me as a former classmate in high school. They wouldn't be able to name any classes I'd taken with them, or the grade I was supposed to be in, but they at least knew my face because they'd interacted with me before.

"Hi," I said.

Liana bit her lip. She was not happy to see me.

Well, what did I expect? I'd crashed into her life, then out of it. Neither had been what she'd wanted at the time.

Gina looked from Liana to me and back, then did what she always did, took charge. "We're going to take boxes down to the car."

Amy complied—people usually did when Gina barked orders.

A moment later they were bustling through the door with plastic bins hefted in their arms. They each gave me a nod on their way past.

Liana retreated to the middle of the room, hands clutched awkwardly, eyes full of questions.

Those eyes.

I slipped inside and shut the door behind me, like a guilty man facing his executioner.

The place had been stripped bare. Grungy white walls with little smudges where posters had been tacked up and a bare mattress stacked with boxes were all that remained. The closet door was open, revealing an assortment of empty hangers. Hints of Febreeze and Pine Sol hung in the air. Now that Liana's friends had left, the room was clear of emotion. Liana knew how to block me and my kind from feeling what she felt, and that alone steadied me. I took a deeper breath. "Hi," I repeated.

"What are you doing here?" Her eyes were wide and her face pale. She caught herself. "Not that I'm not happy to see you. I am. Does the order know you're here?"

"Someone from the order sent me."

She blinked in surprise. "Oh…" A mix of emotions flickered across her features until she settled on confusion once more, then concern. "How are you? Are you okay?"

"My powers came back," I said.

A shadow stole the light from her eyes, but she banished it at once. Did I imagine it, or did her gaze drop to my lips for a split second? Did she regret that I couldn't greet her with another kiss? That I couldn't touch her at all without causing us both severe pain?

Stop, I ordered myself. These musings were pointless now. I was what I was, and no amount of love for Liana would change the moral laws of the universe and let me touch her. I needed to be grateful for the one time I had kissed her, not mooning around like some lovesick teenager wanting more. I was far too old for that.

She took a deep breath, and when she let it out, her shoulders had relaxed a notch. "So it's safe for you to see me again?"

Hardly, I thought. But what I said was, "You're in danger. Darissa's sister has figured out that she's dead."

Liana's eyes widened, then she looked away from me.

"I'm here to protect you," I said.

"Just you? Sorry!" she caught herself. "I didn't mean to imply—"

"The last time you saw me try to fight a vampire I almost got myself killed," I said. "I wouldn't be thrilled either if I were you."

She laughed, nervously, then started to pace, shoes tapping softly on the hard floor. "Please don't tell me it's just you and me against one of the Nabatean vampires again. I mean, I know it worked out last time, but that was a fluke."

"It wasn't a fluke," I said. "You're brilliant. As for whether it's just you and me, it's not. The order is fully committed to taking out Melanie."

"That's the sister's name?" Her gaze darted back to my face.

I nodded. "The last name we have on file for her." There was no telling what the Nabatean sisters' original names were, other than Gamlat's. The other two had adopted whatever new ones suited their purposes down through the ages. "Melanie" was fitting because it meant "dark one."

"Okay," said Liana. "The order's committed to taking her out, sure. But protecting me? They don't really care about that, do they?"

I didn't know whether to be angry or ashamed. Again, she saw way too much. "Don't say that. The order protects human souls, okay? It's what we're for."

Liana stopped pacing and looked at me, actually looked.

I let myself be examined. What could I say? I knew I cut a pathetic figure, a once great immortal brought low, looking ragged and hollow.

"If you don't want to be here—" she began.

"I want to be here. Believe me. Nobody cares about you more than I do."

She lifted an eyebrow.

"I don't mean to imply… anything…"

"You sure you're okay?"

"I'm not myself. It's a long story."

"Will you tell it to me?"

"There's a lot I can't tell you." That answer wasn't fair to her at all.

But if there was one thing Liana understood, it was that life wasn't fair. "Okay," she agreed. She looked aside for a moment, then said, "It is good to see you again. Especially if you're not defying the order to do it."

"Yes… well… I prefer keeping my promise this way."

"And I'm glad you recovered from… you know…"

I pushed my hands deeper into my pockets. "How have you been?"

"Good, I think. I mean… I ended up getting a degree in biology."

"Oh yeah?"

"And I'm not sure what to do with it. It doesn't really go with becoming a hedge fund manager. I don't even know what I'm doing this summer or next year or… if I'm going to grad school." She shrugged, helplessly. "How about you?"

"I've just been working," I said. "Spent a lot of time in refugee camps in Africa. Saw the ruins of buildings I remember from the Roman Empire."

She smiled, but it was a tense smile. I got the sense that this wasn't what she wanted to talk about, but I didn't converse with humans enough to know how to guide the topic elsewhere. I wasn't ever a friend to humans, only their counsellor and guide through the rough patches of life. Even humans who knew what I was let me fill that role, but Liana's situation drew me in deeper. I couldn't just rattle off one-sided lectures at her and expect her to be satisfied with my accumulated wisdom.

I went quiet and hoped she'd consider the ball in her court. And that she'd pick it up and toss it to me rather than let it lie at her feet. If we were going to be spending a lot of time together, I needed all the help I could get.

She folded her arms, then put her hands in her pockets, then shrugged awkwardly.

"So we're talking really loud," came Gina's voice from the hallway. "Because that's a totally normal thing to do. Oh look, we're at Liana's door. We're going to open it now."

Even with warning, I don't think I was able to wipe the guilty look off my face. Liana's friends leaned in with expectant smiles, which immediately dropped into disappointed frowns. It didn't take a mind-reader to see that Liana and I were squared off, awkward in each other's presence. Though I did wonder, what had her friends expected?

Best to just change the subject, fast. "So how have you guys been?" I asked, conversationally.

Out of the corner of my eye, I saw Liana steal over to sit on her bed and make herself look busy, packing.

"We're fine," said Gina. "Let's talk about you."

She had always been hard to work with. Like Liana, she had a mind all her own.

Amy shut the door firmly, stepped out from behind Gina, and the two of them folded their arms.

Okay, now I was confused. Was I about to be lectured? Had Liana been heartbroken after I left? Were they about to tell me all about how hard it had been for her? Dare I hope?

"Let's talk about you being a member of some mysterious religious order," said Gina.

"Yeah," said Amy. "And why don't you explain what exactly you're supposed to be doing here. Helping Liana in some way?"

Liana had told them about the angelic order? I shot her a questioning glance, but her face was blank with utter shock.

She hadn't told them.

Who had, then?

"Guys," said Liana. "What are you talking about?"

"We've been working with the order for a couple of years," said Gina. "But we only just found out that you were, too. And we don't get what Corban's role in all this is."

"Yeah," said Amy. "Care to explain?"

Liana looked to me for guidance, but I was as lost as she was. Nobody had told me anything about the order enlisting these two.

THREE

"Back up," Liana said. "You guys are working for the order?"

"We didn't mean to hide it from you," said Amy. "There just hasn't been a good time to bring it up."

"They did *not* tell me that they had anything to do with you, or with Amy or anything," said Gina. "Siobhan recruited me."

Siobhan—pronounced "Shi-VON"—was probably Siobhan O'Callen, a six hundred year old angel who was lethal in a dagger fight. She held the record for the most hand-to-hand vampire kills by such a wide margin that most of the rest of us didn't bother to keep track anymore. I'd helped her ascend, after I found her living on her own, a widowed young woman in Ireland that no village would take in because of her wild appearance and beliefs about bloodsucking immortals killing her husband. Last I'd known, she'd been working in Britain.

"Siobhan's been living in my house," Liana explained to me. "You know her?"

I nodded.

"Gina's been living there, too," she added.

"Yeah… I kind of got thrown out of my home," said Gina, "and Liana totally saved me. Gave me a place to live and set up my jeweler's bench and my weaponsmithing equipment and all that—"

"Weaponsmithing?" I asked. Gina was a jeweler. A New Mexican, turquoise and silver, southwestern jeweler. Surely she couldn't have gone from jewelry making to—

She pulled a velvet box from her pocket and popped it open to reveal three plain metal rings. They looked like silver, but I knew better.

My stomach tied itself into a knot and I clenched my teeth. *No*, I thought.

"Here, you better wear these," she said, crossing over to Liana and slipping them onto her fingers.

Liana's eyes went misty as she admired them. "These are beautiful! You didn't have to."

"She made some for me too," said Amy, holding up her hands. She also had three.

Gina didn't give me time to wallow in my confusion, though. She'd slipped over to the corner of the room and peeled back the vinyl flooring.

That better not be— I thought

But it was. She held up a small metal amulet. "I put these in the four corners of your room," she said. "Siobhan said they would guard you against evil, even if you invited it in."

"Did she say what kind of evil?" I asked.

"Um… demons?" Gina put the amulet back. "People possessed by demons? Siobhan's weird, okay? But she's nice to me and she's helped me get tons of accounts for my jewelry business. I think she thinks that because we're both Catholic we'll have a lot in common. I mean, we do *technically* believe in demons, and my community in New Mexico does make wards against evil… but… these are new."

I couldn't hold it in any longer. "She should not have had you working with ferrum without telling you what it was."

"She told me," said Gina.

"Ferrum?" asked Liana. She looked at the rings on her fingers again. "You mean iron? That's Latin for iron."

"These are iron?" asked Amy, admiring her hands again.

"What," I demanded from Gina, "did Siobhan tell you, exactly."

"That it's a sacred metal," she said. "Only people of a certain bloodline can work it, and I know that sounds totally messed up." Her glance to each of her friends begged them to hear her out. "But I've seen it. Anyone else tries to work ferrum and it shatters, even if they use my same tools. That's also why my dad didn't want me to learn metalsmithing. I know he said that he didn't want me to be a jeweler, but the truth is that he didn't want me to find out about this family secret, that we're of some kind of bloodline…" Her voice trailed off. There was only so much strangeness any mortal could utter before they lost their nerve. "Anyway." She shrugged.

But everything she'd said was dead on. Ferrum was a sacred metal; there wasn't much of it left in the world. Only members of a certain bloodline could work it, but because they were all human and mortal, the order had decided to stop working with them centuries ago. It wasn't right to put mortals on the front lines of our supernatural war between good and evil. They were already on the front lines of their own.

The bloodline was also old enough that its progeny was legion. One of the early conquistadors who'd explored New Mexico had belonged to it.

My dagger was ferrum, and those amulets, also worked from ferrum, did indeed prevent vampires from entering a room even if they were invited. The order didn't have many of those, and I owed Siobhan big-time for finding out how to get a set installed in Liana's room.

That didn't make any of this right, though.

Liana sensed that her friend didn't want to say anything more, and so turned to Amy. "What'd the order have you do for them?"

"Research," she said, "on this civilization in the ancient Middle East. They were called the Nabateans, and since I did my senior thesis on cave dwellers, it dovetailed. The Nabateans—"

"Built Petra in Jordan," said Liana. "I know who they were."

"Right," said Amy, "so this group came to me my junior year to offer me access to these insane archives. I mean, they had *all* this stuff from that era. Tax records, trade ledgers, census reports."

Liana turned a baleful gaze in my direction, which was fair. "The order doesn't have its own anthropologists? They have to hire my best friend while she's still in undergrad? Why not just paint a target on her forehead?"

I couldn't answer that question off the top of my head. The order didn't have any anthropologists left after Darissa's attacks. Perhaps the order had marked Amy for ascent later in her life, or perhaps different angels with different agendas had each done whatever they thought was right. We were still in such disarray that I couldn't say for sure.

"Okay... what?" asked Amy. "So, um, right before I came out here for your graduation, my contact with the order told me that Gina and Liana also worked for them, that I should be ready to leave straight from here to do field work in Turkey, and that I'd be getting some kind of briefing today. At Liana's house in Southampton. It was... I kind of wondered if I'd gotten involved in organized crime? Or something?" Her voice went pitchy with uncertainty. "Please tell me it isn't organized crime. I just did research on cave dwellers, I swear."

"Or a cult," said Gina. "It's not a cult, is it? And Corban, why are you involved with them?"

"How did you guys know Corban was involved?" Liana asked.

"Siobhan texted me," said Gina. "Guys, seriously, tell us what's going on. I mean, I thought this was weird when I was just learning how to forge daggers out of sacred metal."

"And I had no idea that was happening," said Amy, her hand up, palm out. "I seriously just thought it was some well-endowed foundation with a whole lot of Nabatean artifacts."

Liana looked askance at me, but I wasn't prepared to deal with this. "Tell them whatever you think they need to know," I said. I trusted her judgment. The order had put her in this situation, after all. They would have to suffer whatever consequences resulted.

She bit her lip and turned her knees and toes in, sitting awkwardly on the edge of her bed. "Okay…" she said. "Um, so the order isn't religious *exactly*. It endorses a lot of religions. It's not, like, a Christian religious order or a Muslim one or anything like that."

"What is it, then?" asked Gina.

"It's… an ancient secret society that fights… um… well. Demons."

"Actual demons?" asked Gina.

"Yeah, actual demons. Specifically vampires." She bit her lip again.

Gina blinked, turning her attention inward to digest that.

Amy, however, perked up. "What kind of vampires? Like the Eastern European kind? The bloodsucking, sexy ones?" Just like every other scholar I'd met down through the ages, she was ever curious, willing to follow trails of facts into mortal danger and beyond. I tried not to shake my head in dismay.

"Yeah," said Liana. "Those are the ones. And I get if that sounds totally insane."

But Amy only shrugged. "Look, you don't have to explain to me that not everyone lives in the same reality. Legend and beliefs underpin everyone's worldview. My people believe a lot of things that would sound pretty strange to you."

This was probably accurate. I hadn't ever used my veil to spy on Amy's Red Willow People. All I knew was that they were an indigenous tribe that still retained a lot of their ancestral beliefs and practices, and did not share them with the outside world. They held fast to their heritage after weathering the apocalyptic fallout of European colonization. When I'd been a Roman, I'd believed that the people we'd conquered were barbarians in need of civilizing. It was a belief that our cultural/linguistic descendents had to unlearn as they spread their own empires across the world. Every time I looked at Amy, I wondered how many cultures had been lost to the cause of "civilizing" them. The tally I was personally aware of was far too high, and a bottomless well of shame for me.

Gina had also started to nod. "I know I said Siobhan's Catholicism is weird, but so is mine. I mean, not everything my family does would be specifically endorsed by the Vatican."

Liana looked surprised.

Well, that made sense. Liana was steeped in America's mainstream culture. It probably hadn't occurred to her that balancing her existence as a vampire with being a regular American college student was somewhat akin to her friends also having separate public and personal cultures, different faces they showed in different situations. Liana was a much less extreme version of the person I'd been, and people I'd known, as a Roman. While we'd been supremacists, she was merely unaware.

"You actually seen any vampires?" Gina asked.

"I am one," Liana confessed. "But… it's kind of complicated."

Amy and Gina exchanged an uncertain look. Then they looked at the sunlight streaming in through the windows, and Liana's reflection in the mirror mounted on the wall. Their gazes took in her healthy, rosy glow. I couldn't read their minds, but I could get the gist. She didn't look like any vampire they'd ever heard of.

Gina barked a laugh. "Sure, *now* it's complicated."

FOUR

Gina stared at the ferrum rings on Liana's fingers. "So ferrum doesn't actually work on vampires?"

"What's it supposed to do?" Amy asked.

"Burn them," said Gina. "Siobhan said that if I wore the rings and used my hands to block an attack, I could at least sting a vampire."

"I'm not fully turned," said Liana. "That's what's complicated. I'm infected with vampirism, but I'm not a full vampire."

"How common is that?" Amy was *all* into this conversation. Normally Gina was the chatty one.

"It's never happened before," I said. "Ever."

"I don't know about that." Liana shot me a look of strained patience. "The order hasn't ever seen it before."

"So Corban you are…?" Gina turned to me, one eyebrow lifted in query.

"A vampire hunter," I filled in. "That's what I was doing at Taos High, and that's why you barely ever saw me going to classes and stuff. The principal thought I was a narc." I'd given Liana carte blanche, so if she wanted to tell her friends that there was more to my story, this was her chance.

But she didn't. All she said was, "Yeah, he found me on the first day of school, cornered me in the bathroom, told me he was going to kill me." She shrugged.

"Which was wrong of me," I was quick to point out. I didn't want her friends to get the wrong idea. "I took it back."

"So how'd you get infected?" Amy asked, ignoring me.

"Ex-boyfriend." Liana wrung her hands. "Well, I dunno if he counted as a boyfriend. He was a mistake."

"Talk about the STD from hell," said Gina.

"Literally," Amy agreed.

"I didn't sleep with him."

"That just makes it worse," said Gina. "How do you get infected?"

"It's a bite-bit thing, right?" Amy asked. "They bite you and you bite them." At Gina and Liana's surprised looks she shrugged. "I like reading vampire novels, all right? It's called a guilty pleasure. People have those."

"I thought you just liked reading anthropology textbooks," said Gina.

"So now you know my deep dark secret. Use it for good, not evil," she fired back.

"It is a bite-bit thing," said Liana. "I thought I was in love and that we'd be together forever. I was stupid, okay?"

"I dunno, was he sexy?" asked Amy. "Some of those vampire bad boys—"

"He was an abusive monster," I said. "That should not make him sexy."

Now Amy had her hands up in surrender.

I needed to dial it back.

"Anyhow," Liana said, "what's in Turkey? Amy's contact with the order said she's supposed to go to Turkey. You were in Turkey after… the last time we talked."

After the first and last time we'd kissed.

"Our headquarters," I said. "And our full archives," I added for Amy's benefit. "Most libraries have a card catalog and shelving numbers? Ours has a tram system."

"So my friends can go there and be safe?" Liana asked.

"A tram system?" Amy's eyes were wide. Getting her to go wouldn't be hard.

"Yeah," I said. "I'm guessing that's the plan."

"Wait, be safe from what?" Gina asked Liana. "Are you going to turn into a full vampire and hurt us?"

"I hope not." Liana frowned.

"She killed one of the oldest and most powerful vampires in all of history," I said. "Now another ancient, powerful vampire wants revenge."

"I got lucky," said Liana. "She was gonna kill me. I killed her first."

"When?" Gina asked.

"Senior year." Liana shrugged, as if this were all no big deal.

Her friends gaped at her.

She began to drum her heels against the floor, a clear plea for someone to change the subject.

I hid a smile. "The order can protect you guys." Gina and Amy were unambiguously human, and my kind would do anything to keep them safe. "Gina, did Siobhan tell you that ferrum workers can be made immune to vampires?"

Gina shrugged. "She started talking about some ritual thing and… I didn't want to hear it."

"Okay, well she was probably talking about turning the iron in your blood to ferrum. Amy, you're in the bloodline too, so this'll work on you as well. You guys okay with me doing this?"

Liana perked up. "What's the ritual involve?"

"I give you each a small cut with a ferrum dagger. It'll heal immediately."

"That's it?" said Gina.

"That's it."

"Well I feel kind of stupid now."

"Don't," I said. "And don't let people cut you as a general rule, all right?"

"Whatever." She rolled her eyes. "You're not the boss of me." She held out her arm, wrist up.

Amy did the same.

I drew my dagger, which involved a sleight of hand maneuver that made them both jerk in surprise. "It's… the sheath is here." I pushed my sleeve up so they could see. "I didn't do anything magical."

They stood still as I nicked them each in the upper arm, where there were fewer nerve endings. A quick touch of my fingers healed their cuts at once and only stung me a little. That was the thing about my current condition. My healing powers were potent. "And we're done," I said. "To vampires, you smell like poison and are poison. You won't get bitten, but this doesn't mean you can't still be kidnapped or tortured or any of that, so you still need to let the order protect you."

Gina, who was still rubbing her arm, nodded. "Got it."

"Yep," Amy agreed. "Let's make a move to the house, guys. See if Siobhan can explain to us what we do next. Me and Gina in her car and you and Corban in your car?" She looked at Liana for confirmation.

But I was the one who spoke up. Time alone with Liana? It was a terrible idea and odds were I'd be getting too much of that anyway.

"Yeah," I said. "Sounds good."

"DO *NOT* LAUGH," Liana ordered me as we approached her car with armloads of boxes. The sun was high, the sky cloudless, and the day bright.

If I could have obeyed her, I would have, but I couldn't. I cracked up. She had my old car, my old turquoise RAV4 with the scratch on the back fender and everything.

"I got it cheap at a police auction," she said, dropping her boxes on the ground so that she could open the back hatch.

Gina and Amy were with Gina's car, which was parked right in front of Liana's dorm. At least I wasn't embarrassing Liana in front of them.

I really needed to stop laughing, but it was hard. I managed to for long enough to ask, "Are you any better at driving it?"

In response Liana turned and flung the keys at my chest. I managed to catch them, but it stung a bit.

"You're driving it," she said. "You don't have to sleep."

"Okay, okay."

I edged her aside and loaded the boxes in the back of the car. She flipped her hair over her shoulder and went to climb into the passenger seat. Between the four of us, we'd managed to carry all the boxes out of her dorm room and Liana had turned in her keys. She'd given her room one last wistful look, and then finished yet another milestone on the way to adulthood.

Once I had the boxes loaded and closed the back hatch with the a metallic thud, I paused a moment to collect my wits. I'd missed this little mini-SUV; it'd been mine for years.

A light breeze had picked up, which didn't make the air any less heavy and oppressive. I preferred dry climates.

Liana didn't move as I got into the driver's seat, and didn't look at me until I shut the door and clicked my seatbelt on. Her expression was pure apprehension.

This was going to continue to be awkward. Perhaps it was best if I just ripped the band-aid off. "Can I ask you some questions?"

"Yeah…" Her expression was wary.

"Are you dating anyone? I need to know who else besides Gina and Amy could be used against you." *Stay. Calm.* I ordered myself. Liana wasn't mine. She was supposed to date other people.

She rolled her eyes. "No."

Traitorous hope blossomed in me. "I'm just asking."

"I never got over you, okay?" She flung the words in my face with more force than she'd thrown the keys. "Go ahead and laugh. I'm the pathetic mortal girl who can't get over being kissed by an angel."

The band-aid was definitely off. "I'd never laugh at you."

"You laugh at me all the time. You laughed at the car—"

"I did not mean it like that! I just thought it was funny that you bought the car that you stole from me that one time."

"That you made me drive without a license, oh heavenly one?"

"Right. Lots of memories." I patted the steering wheel. "I'd never laugh at ruining your love life, okay? That wasn't what I wanted to do." Except that I kind of did. I shut my eyes and scrubbed my face with my hands. How to phrase this?

When I looked up again, though, Liana had her back to me. "Just drive," she said.

This conversation wasn't over, but maybe better words would come to me with a little time. I started the car.

Something in the way Liana adjusted her posture let me know, she wasn't happy I'd done what she'd asked. I was so bad at this.

LIANA SLEPT THE entire drive from Princeton to Southampton, stirring once when an ambulance went screaming past in New York City.

This gave me time to think about what to say next, but even as I turned onto her street in Southampton, my mind was blank. Agonizing over what to say had distracted me from my usual hunger to hurt people so that I could gorge on their pain, at least; but I was here to help her, not me.

Liana's neighborhood was full of mansions set back among mature trees on acre lots. I had to slow down to follow the instructions on my phone's GPS, since Gina was behind me in her little red sedan. She and Amy were cracking up at something, a stark contrast to the ringing silence inside the RAV4.

Please, I prayed, *Lord, help me out here.*

A blinding flash up ahead turned my vision white, then red, then dim. I could see the street ahead once more, but it was as if I'd walked into a dark house on a bright summer's day. I felt more than heard the blast.

Liana jerked awake and sat up. "What was that?"

"God having a sense of humor?" I said. "Well, not really."

A great cloud of smoke was billowing up from behind the trees on our right.

"What?" She twisted around to face me.

"Pretty sure someone just blew up your house. I totally should not have made a joke about that."

FIVE

Liana was right that I had laughed at her all the time. She was the kind of mortal who saw the world as it was. It wasn't that I thought she was funny, but rather that she was right. The world was what was funny… sometimes.

I'd also fantasized that we really were friends, despite our differences. I couldn't hide from her. We'd saved each other's lives and gone out for burgers—and there was no one else that I could say both of those things about.

Now I was pretty sure our friendship was over. Every laugh, every joke I made about her, all of that was coming back to haunt me.

I'd pulled the RAV4 over to the side of the road while Liana sobbed.

"Sorry," I said with as much sincerity as I could. I did care. I was just not good at showing it.

Siobhan strode up the sidewalk, waving cheekily. Her dark hair fell in ringlet curls and her skin was like fine china. I had an urge to throw my dagger through the window, right into her heart. I wouldn't even open the window first. Let her get stabbed with my dagger *and* shards of flying glass.

But I didn't have time for petty revenge either. Siobhan was holding up a set of license plates, and I needed to get those onto Liana's car. The RAV4 still had a yellow and red New Mexico plate, and those were far too easy to recognize, even at great distance.

I vaulted out of my seat and jogged around the car, only to find Siobhan had already unscrewed the back license plate and was putting on a New York plate in its place. The air smelled of acrid smoke and I could dimly sense the rising panic of people up and down the street who were starting to realize what had happened. Fortunately, they were all a good distance away. I caught their fear like I might catch a whiff of wildflowers if the field were a hundred yards away. It was mild. Nothing registered from Liana. She had her walls up even now.

"Relax," Siobhan said in her Irish brogue—carefully cultivated down the centuries to keep up with the times. "It's all under control."

"Excuse me?"

She straightened up and marched around the passenger side of the car with the other license plate tucked under her arm. Her stiletto heels clacked against the asphalt and I did not understand how she kept her balance in those and a tight pencil skirt. Then again, she'd had hundreds of years of practice.

I charged after her, but had nothing to do once we reached the front of the car besides stand over her while she installed the plate. A smile was playing at the corners of her mouth and she took her time to straighten up and face me.

A police car screamed past, ignoring us and speeding around the corner.

"Right on time," said Siobhan.

"Tell me you didn't blow up Liana's house."

"Oh don't be silly. Of course not. That was Melanie. Quite the campaign she put together to find the place. We're going to make it look like a dead end, all right? At the very least we'll delay her long enough to get Liana and her friends to Turkey."

Gina's little red sedan pulled up behind us and Amy was out the door before it had made a complete stop. Her face was stricken as she stared at the rising column of smoke. "L—" she began to shout.

I made a cutting motion to silence her. "No names," I said. "No identifying information, we clear? Get in the RAV."

She gave me a baffled look, but did what I asked, climbing into the back seat just as Gina darted around the other side of the car to also climb in. Once inside, they both reached out to console Liana, who kept on sobbing, hard enough to form tearstains. That was difficult for a vampire—even a half-turned one.

I turned back to Siobhan.

"You look terrible," she said.

I rolled my eyes. "Explain how having Melanie find Liana's house and blow it up is part of the plan? And having Liana get this close, so Melanie can record video of her face and car? That part of the plan too? How does changing the license plate fix this?"

More police cars screamed past, along with a fire truck and an ambulance. The first police cruiser was back. The officer strung up a makeshift barrier across the street with crime scene tape that flapped in the breeze. Nobody looked our direction because Siobhan and I were standing close enough to the car for our veiling to partly cover it. People might know the car was here, but they would feel compelled to look away.

To vampires the effect was stronger. My kind were simply invisible. Only if we interacted directly with a vamp could it see us. If Melanie or her minions were recording this, they'd have trouble even discerning that the license plates had been changed. But vampires didn't get to be as old and powerful as Melanie without being smart enough to watch and rewatch footage, forcing themselves to see anything they could, even if it was hard.

"Here we go," said Siobhan, looking past me. "Liana's taken care of."

I turned to see a black Cadillac with dark tinted windows pull up next to Liana's car.

"What? You hired the mob to take her out?"

Siobhan elbowed me in the ribs, hard. "That's her lawyer."

Sure enough, a man with silvery hair and an expensive suit climbed out and went to tap on Liana's window.

She rolled it down, wiping her tears away with a tissue. "Hey."

"You have the combo to my beach house, right?" he asked her. "You go there, okay? Stay as long as you need."

"I can—"

"Liana," he said, "I know you can take care of yourself. Take a break, kiddo." He had the air of a distraught yet proud grandfather, taking his high achieving granddaughter to task. It made sense. He'd no doubt seen rich kids orphaned before. Most struggled to manage the money they inherited and the sudden freedoms that came with it. Liana was an exception. She had kept on plugging away at school and had gotten a degree from an Ivy League university right on schedule. Her major crisis at the moment was not knowing whether to go to grad school or straight into the workforce.

For a family lawyer, she was a dream client.

He reached through the window and put his hands on her shoulders. "Just go there, okay? I'll talk to the cops and all that. We'll deal with this." He gestured in the direction of the smoke.

Just then the wind changed direction and brought with it the reek of burning wood, plastic, and other smells that I could only classify as "burning house." It was very different from the smell of a forest fire or brush fire.

In this case it was the scent of Liana's childhood memories up in smoke.

"Get her out of here," Siobhan ordered me. "We'll meet up at the beach house."

Liana nodded at her lawyer, tears still streaking down her cheeks. He patted her on the shoulder before pulling back. "I'll be in touch soon," he promised her.

I went around to get back into the driver's seat and put the car in gear. The street was now a maze of emergency vehicles, the lawyer's car, and one poor sedan trying to worm its way through. The police were waving at it to turn around.

"How do I get to the beach house?" I asked, feeling like a heel to interfere with Liana's grief with such a pedestrian question.

She tapped the address into her phone and handed it to me.

THE BEACH HOUSE was only a mile and a half away. Here the air smelled briny, and seagulls screamed overhead. The house itself was picture perfect, painted a distinguished shade of slate gray with white trim.

Liana climbed out of the car and punched the code into the keypad on the door, then she and her friends went in, and I followed, locking the door behind me with an audible thunk.

The girls went straight to the sitting room, with its large picture windows that showed gray-blue waves crashing on the sandy beach. A few people were strolling along the shoreline, including a family with a little girl who was trying to eat a popsicle and walk at the same time.

I was only surveying the scene to figure out whether or not Liana could be spied on here. I went and lowered the blinds and then made a quick circuit of the house, making sure all the doors were locked and windows closed.

When I returned, Liana was still sitting in the middle of the couch with her two friends hugging her. I owed her an apology, but now wasn't the best time. What I did say was, "You should be safe for now."

And that lifted my veil for Amy and Gina.

Both looked up at me. "What happened?" Gina asked. "Did vampires blow up her house? I can't believe I just said that…"

Amy started to crack up, and to my surprise, Liana joined in. She'd just lost everything left to her by her father, and she was able to laugh? Humans were crazy resilient.

"No," said Gina. "I had those amulet thingies in the house too, and it's daytime. How could vampires even get in?"

"By hiring humans," I said. "Vampires don't do their own dirty work if they can avoid it."

Liana wouldn't look at me. I had no one to blame but myself for that.

The front door opened. "Knock, knock," said Siobhan. She came clacking into the room, looking like she'd just come from an art gallery exhibition. "Everyone all right?" she asked.

"Explain what's going on, now," I ordered. "You sure you have a plan to deal with all this?"

SIX

Siobhan lifted an eyebrow at me, pushing back against my demands.

The right thing to do was be conciliatory. That was the angelic way, but fury continued to build in me like steam in a plugged-up kettle. I had to take a few deep breaths to calm down.

I drew myself up to my full height and squared my shoulders.

Siobhan reached into her purse and came up with a passport, which she handed to Gina. "I wasn't able to get much out of the house before it blew, but I did manage this. I know this is a lot to ask but—"

"You want me to go to Turkey." Gina shrugged as if this were no big deal.

"We already talked about it," I said. "Because apparently you've already recruited Gina to work ferrum for us."

"Yes, well," said Siobhan, "we did get the ferrum out of the house before it blew. Much as I would like watching vampires try to deal with particles of ferrum all over the place, the stuff is too valuable."

"Right," I snapped, "because that's what I care about, you moving the ferrum supply! Excuse me, but Gina's a mortal and you don't just drag her into our war because you want some charms made."

Siobhan winced away from me and Gina and Amy's expressions were stricken. They might not have known me well, but they knew I didn't typically blow up like that.

Only Liana seemed unfazed by it. "What he said," was her reaction. She folded her arms across her chest.

"Yeah," said Siobhan, "well all that progress we made, killing off all vampires besides the Nabatean sisters? It doesn't matter. Melanie turned over two hundred people in Southampton last night and sent them out door-to-door, claiming they were buying a house in the neighborhood and wanted to know how safe it was. She located Liana's house as the scene where Darissa assassinated Liana's father within an hour. I was out half the night rounding up baby vampires, and I'm not sure I got all of them."

Now, this was very, very bad. Vampires were usually rare, because my order was good at killing them, but they could spread like the outbreak of a virus. It only took one vampire to pose a serious risk to humanity.

"You'll be happy to know I just put them all in a room and tried to get them through sunrise. None of them made it." Siobhan shrugged. "So that's a lot of cover stories to concoct for families."

"This isn't what I care about," I said. "I'm here to protect Liana. Once vampires were loose, why did you let them get far enough to find and then blow up her house?"

"So that Melanie won't figure out that our order is protecting the owner of that house. It's one thing for there to have been a murder there. If it's obvious that we're watching over the property, then Melanie will know for sure that Liana is who she's looking for."

It was like the old World War II tactic used by the Allies after they cracked the Axis enigma machine. For two years the Allies were able to read all the encoded German communiques, but if they'd let on that they'd cracked the code, the Germans would have changed it. The Allies had let a lot of ships get sunk and towns get bombed in order to keep that advantage. It was a cold analysis, reserved for war.

This decision was personal to Liana, and that made it personal to me. I knew better than to push that point with Siobhan, though. My kind cared about souls, not things. My emotional reaction was petty and small.

"Before the bomb went off," Siobhan explained, standing with her body angled to address everyone present—the three girls on the couch and me standing with my arms folded. "We swept the neighborhood. Nobody got any video of Liana's car pulling up. The place has been crawling with members of the order since the wee hours of this morning. We should plan for Melanie to figure out that Liana didn't die in that explosion, though. There were also some hitmen there with sniper rifles who'll have a hard time remembering what happened. We can't expect our ruse to hold up forever. I say we've got two days' head start."

I pressed my hands to my face. "Okay…" I muttered. "Explain to me why Melanie won't know she's on the right track already? She's figured out that the police records about Liana's father's murder were altered. Who besides us alters police records?"

"Rich people who are paranoid," said Siobhan. "We hired human companies, lawyers—the whole ball of wax—to hide that paper trail. If Melanie figures out how it was done, she'll only know that Liana's rich and afraid of being killed by whoever took out her father."

"And if she doesn't take the time to chase down all those details?" I responded. "Come on, it's our typical playbook, altering records. She'll know."

"Well, we'll get everyone out of here in short order and it won't matter if Melanie knows. We'll be several steps ahead of her."

The full meaning of this struck Liana at once. "You mean we're leaving the country right now?" That meant not seeing her home, or what was left of it. It meant not getting time to deal until she was on a plane over the Atlantic.

"Okay," said Gina. "That's fine by me."

"Me too," Amy agreed.

Liana hesitated. "But… if Melanie's found me, she'll know Cassie is my only living family." Cassie, her aunt and guardian until she'd turned eighteen, lived alone out in New Mexico. She would be a perfect target.

"I've got a coterie on its way here to escort the girls," said Siobhan. "Also, this house has a bolthole." She held up her phone. It showed a diagram of a tunnel out of the house that led to the storm drain. "Not that we'll need it. We'll get you girls to safety."

"What about all of Liana's things loaded into the cars?" I asked. "We'll need to lock them away somewhere that Melanie's not going to find them."

"Yes, that's easy."

"You're sure about that?"

Siobhan looked me over. "You sure you're all right?"

"No, of course I'm not all right. But there's no time to worry about that."

As if to prove my point, a car pulled up into the driveway.

I went to the front room and peered out a window. The car was a white luxury sedan that didn't belong to Liana's lawyer, and didn't appear to be one of ours.

Siobhan had followed me and I gave her a questioning look. "You expecting anyone other than that coterie?"

She shook her head. "Girls!" she called out. "Time to go." To me she said, "Help me veil them."

Liana and her friends came piling into the entryway.

I pointed to the door to the closet under the stairs. "Go in there," I told Liana. "Give Siobhan your cell phone first."

Without batting an eye, she handed over her cell phone, then went and shut herself in, the latch sliding into place with a soft click.

Siobhan put a hand on Gina's shoulder and I did the same to Amy. Fortunately they were both wearing cap sleeves, so it was easy to get a grip on them without risking skin-to-skin contact.

"We're going to escort you out to Gina's car," Siobhan said. "Just stay with us and do what we say. No one's going to start a firefight in broad daylight in public."

"And don't ever try this on your own," I said.

These two wouldn't understand that the bad guys couldn't see them.

Amy was shaking with nerves so badly that I feared she'd faint, but she made it down the walk to the street and the waiting car. I helped her into the back seat of Gina's sedan. The fact that Gina had parked in the street, rather than the driveway, was fortuitous. The white car, which was now disgorging three men who looked like they meant business, wasn't blocking them in.

I had to push some of the boxes in the backseat over—boxes of Liana's things. How was I going to fit Liana in here?

Gina rode shotgun and Siobhan dashed around to the driver's seat.

There came the sound of glass breaking behind me. Sickness coiled around my stomach as I turned. The three men had broken the windows of the RAV4 and one of them was holding aloft a sheet of paper. My guess? Her car registration.

To Siobhan I said, "Throw me your keys." Which she did, pitching them from the driver's seat to where I leaned in through the passenger rear door. I caught them one-handed, pocketed them, and stepped back. "Take them to the airport. I'll take care of Liana."

"All right," said Siobhan. "Good luck." She started the car and drove away, leaving her own Subaru parked across the road.

The men in the driveway showed no sign of being able to see me as I headed back into the house. I closed and locked the front door behind me before I went to open the closet. Liana sat on the floor in the dark, her knees drawn up to her chest, her eyes wide and scared. "What do I do now?"

"Random question," I said. "What address is on your car registration?"

Her eyes went wide. "It's got Cassie's address." Fresh tears began to slip down her cheeks. "Did they break into my car? I'm so sorry."

"Liana," I said, "you just had your house blown up and are running for your life. I didn't think to take your registration out of the car either."

"But my aunt!"

"It's all right. We'll find a way to keep her safe."

Someone began beating on the front door and I ducked into the closet and pulled the door shut behind me, plunging us both into darkness. I was keenly aware of Liana, though, of the heat radiating off her body and the sound of her breathing, of the fact that I could reach out a hand and clasp her shoulder, though I didn't.

Focus, I ordered myself. "We're leaving the house through that bolthole, all right?"

SEVEN

I pulled out my cell phone for light. Not the flashlight—as that would obliterate our night sight. The screen light would have to do. Liana's features were ghostly in the dimness, which added to the unreality of this moment.

"The tunnel's here," I explained as I got down on my knees on the hard floor and pulled open the little metal door of the fuse box. With a quick yank I pulled the fuse box out to reveal a tunnel beyond. "You'll have to crabwalk in, and it leads to a shaft that you'll have to climb down. There are ladder rungs."

Liana got onto her knees and peered into the darkness. "Why do you guys have a tunnel in my lawyer's house?"

"I've always pushed for options when it came to taking care of you," I said. "Looks like the order listened. I mean, I hoped this would never be the site of a major showdown with someone like Melanie, but if you look at the odds…" I shrugged. "And Siobhan's got a lot of pull. My guess is this is her handiwork."

"So just because locks don't work on you guys, you feel like you can go into people's homes and install stuff like tunnels?"

How had she figured that out? "Who says locks don't work on us?" I tried to sound noncommittal.

"I heard you lock the front door and Siobhan came waltzing right in."

"Maybe she knows your lawyer?"

"And I remember years ago, you accessing my phone contacts when my screen was locked."

I heaved a sigh. "You remember me using your phone four years ago?"

"Of course I do! You had me cornered in the bathroom and were talking about killing me and I got my phone out to call the police but I dropped it, and you picked it up and started going through it."

"Most people," I pointed out, "wouldn't be paying attention to little details like that when their life is in danger."

"That moment," she said, leaning in, "is seared onto my memory. You traumatized me."

I sensed there was laughter lurking beneath her sternness, though, and that I didn't understand. "Please just get in the tunnel," I said.

"You said crabwalk. That implies I go sideways—"

"Just…" I was frustrated now. "Feet first," I ordered. "Face up. You know what I mean."

The knocking on the front door resumed and Liana scrambled into action, slipping into the narrow tunnel.

I waited a second for her to get all the way in, then followed her while the pounding on the front door intensified. The doorbell rang several times in succession.

I muttered to myself as I squeezed into the dark confines of the tunnel and then twisted so I was on my stomach. This way I could pull the fuse box in and the door shut.

"Don't do that," whisper-shouted Liana from the darkness.

"Do what?" I whisper-shouted back.

"Talk to yourself. Siobhan does that and it drives me insane. When nobody else sees her? It makes me look like a crazy person."

"Sorry," I said. I got the hatch shut and carefully maneuvered the fuse box into place, its metal edges digging into my fingers. It slipped home with a metallic click.

A muffled bang in the house was probably the front door being kicked in. "Did you leave anything in the sitting room?" I asked, switching off my phone to plunge us into pitch darkness.

"N-no... I wasn't carrying anything."

"Okay, well they'll still take some time to search the house, I think. Maybe they'll think you sneaked out the back door."

"I mean, I have my prepaid credit cards on me. I put those in my moneybelt when I was packing up my room."

"You're wearing a moneybelt?" I asked.

"Yeah, with cash and cards and my passport. I'm paranoid, okay?"

I started to laugh, but stifled it as best I could. "This proves you are not paranoid."

"I didn't tape a flashlight to my body, though. Do you have a flashlight?" Her voice was getting more distant.

"Yeah, hang on." I fished my keychain out of my pocket and detached the little flashlight. Since there wasn't enough room for me to turn around, I just laid it on the floor and gave it a hard push in the direction of the shaft. "Look out below." I heard the soft pings of the flashlight bouncing off the walls. It was crazy how durable modern technology was.

A soft glow came on, allowing me to see the outline of my feet, and I scrabbled towards the shaft. "You off the ladder?" I asked.

"Yeah." Her soft voice was very distant now. "Lucky for us I'm not claustrophobic, huh?"

"You probably will be after this." It took some interesting contortions to get myself onto the ladder, facing the wall, but I managed it and climbed down towards the glow of the flashlight in the narrow tunnel below. It dimmed steadily as Liana headed off without me.

"Wait!" I whisper-shouted, letting go of the ladder and dropping all the way to the bottom.

The light stopped dimming. I knelt and peered down the hallway that led to the storm drain. Liana was a shadow with a halo.

"You're not scared of the dark, are you?" she whispered.

"Of course I am."

She started to laugh, but stifled it. "No way."

"Hey, I know what goes bump in the night." This tunnel was a little bigger, so I was able to crawl. The hard cement pressed painfully against my knees.

Once she heard me coming, she resumed crawling towards the storm drain.

"Wait for me when you get to the end," I told her, which probably wasn't necessary. What did I think she would do? Take off running without me?

"Roger, roger," she said.

We crawled along until the tunnel opened up into the storm drain, which was dimly lit by daylight from curb cutouts over our heads. Prolific graffiti on the walls showed that plenty of people had passed by here, as did the reek of urine, mixing in with the scents of damp concrete and rotting fish.

Liana stood up, stretched her arms over her head to loosen her joints, and then handed me my flashlight. "Where do we go now?"

"The best thing we can do," I said, "is double back to the house and take Siobhan's car." I held up the keys.

"Do you need keys to start cars?" Liana asked. "How does that work? The ignition is a type of lock, isn't it?"

"No," I said. "Not for my purposes." I did not know why that was. Liana would probably be able to figure it out in five minutes flat, but that was her, not me.

"So are you able to make me invisible when we go back? That's what you did for Amy and Gina, right?" She was chattier now, the silent treatment she'd given me in the car on hold. As I walked, she stayed in step with me.

This was painful in a different way. I think this is what mortal guys would call "feeling friend-zoned."

And despite all the distractions of our current situation, my hunger was now like a black hole that wanted to consume the world. My vision swam with it. What I said, though, was, "Yeah, I should be able to veil you."

Liana's head turned in my direction. "You okay?"

"I'm just tapped out."

"You want my grief? I've got tons."

"No. Thank you. I know you don't want to give that away."

Liana had very little left but her pain. Her father and now her home were gone. While most people collected keepsakes, all she had left was the void that came from a lack of them.

"I'll get some actual food once we get the car." I was relying on that a lot these days. Food took the edge off my constant, insatiable hunger for human pain. "Let's go."

Light up ahead indicated that there was, indeed an opening, and we soon stepped out of the dimness of the tunnel and into the briny air of the beach. The surf crashed in a dull roar and seagulls screamed overhead once more.

Liana looked at me. Her knees and the heels of her hands were grimy and she'd left a smudge of dirt on the side of her nose when she'd touched her face. Her hair was a little extra wild from the exertions of our escape.

She looked like the leading lady of an action movie, gorgeous with superficial scuffs, vulnerable yet strong.

For a moment I tried to imagine what she'd look like without the vampirism. Her face a little fuller, maybe, her waist a little broader. Prettier in a more authentic way. It didn't help at all. I wanted to kiss her again. I wanted to tell her how much I'd missed her. I had no business thinking such thoughts.

"So…" I said, dusting off my hands. "I need to put my hand on your shoulder to veil you. That okay?"

She nodded.

I put my palm against her shoulderblade, feeling the heat of her skin through the fabric of her shirt, then paused. This didn't feel like enough. I wanted to put my arm around her, and although it was rare of my kind to be so familiar, she was in real danger and we were about to go straight into the path of those who would hurt her. "Um, actually," I whispered, slipping my arm around her shoulders.

Her muscles went tense as iron cords and I hated making her feel uncomfortable. I wanted to hate myself for the sense of rightness in my heart as I took her in a half-embrace.

Still, my mind noted the vanilla body wash scent of her skin and her soft curves against my side. It reminded me of the times back in Taos, when she, saving my life, had wrapped her arm around my waist and pressed her body against mine to help me walk.

We looked like a couple to anyone who could see us. But not being seen was the point.

Besides, if I truly loved her, I needed to put her needs first. I needed to find my angelic side again and love selflessly.

Liana stayed rigid, her expression pinched with discomfort.

"Sorry," I whispered, "if this is too forward of me."

"It's fine." She kept her gaze straight ahead.

"Okay, just until we get to the car."

Her nod was curt.

EIGHT

We reached the sidewalk and had to file carefully through a group of teenagers going the other way. They moved around us automatically, but none of them so much as looked at us or said hello.

I was hyperaware of the shift and sway of Liana's body as she walked.

Foot traffic had picked up along the street, which was a very good development. By the time we reached the beach house, there were enough other people milling around that as long as Liana was unremarkable, the guys in the beach house wouldn't take note of her even if they did see her.

Besides, the blinds were still drawn, so they couldn't be looking in our direction. This meant we couldn't see in and discover what they were doing to the house, which was for the best. Liana would feel guilty, even though this was not her fault at all.

I unlocked Siobhan's Subaru Crosstrek with the key fob and helped Liana into the passenger seat. She turned her face away while I went around to the driver's seat and got the engine started.

We'd made it. We were going to get away.

Fifteen minutes later we were parked in the parking lot of a superstore and I was devouring my second cheeseburger while Liana dialed her aunt's number on my phone again.

The car interior was getting rapidly warmer without the AC running, and that brought out the vanilla scent of Liana's skin still more. Was it really a body wash? Or maybe a moisturizer? Both? It wasn't an appropriate line of questioning for me to pursue.

"Hi Cassie," she said.

For a moment I hoped this meant her aunt had answered the call, but that faded when Liana went on to say, "Hey, so I can't give you a number to call back right now. I'll get you one when I can, and I'll call you again later on today, all right?" With a frustrated frown, she ended the call and handed me my phone.

"I'm sorry we can't give her my number," I said.

The look she gave me was sheer annoyance. "That's not the problem. I already left her numbers to call. Lydia's for example. It's not good when she doesn't answer. It's not normal."

"She's always fighting impulses," I pointed out. "Fighting the impulse to pick up her phone could be normal. Especially when the number calling in is blocked." *Corban,* I thought, *don't pretend to be the expert on her aunt.*

I mean, I did know her aunt and had for years. Cassie Linacre had a bad case of OCD, which made her quirky in the best of times and impossible the rest of the time. Liana had lived with her, though.

Liana shrugged. "I get the feeling it's more than that. When I called three times in quick succession, she should have known something was up." As she spoke, she watched me eat with brows drawn together in confusion.

Yes, I was a very different man than I'd been when I saw her last. That version of me could sit benevolently and soak in people's pain, and that had been all the nourishment I needed. Now, I finished my second burger, wiped my fingers on my napkin, and took my phone back from her.

The directory told me who was in charge of Taos these days, an angel named Roberto Morales, I gave him a call.

"Mr. Alexander," he replied with a reverence that disgusted me. Since I'd never met this guy, he had no reason to respect me. All he really knew about me was that I was old.

"Mr. Morales, sorry to bother you. I've been trying to reach Cassie Linacre."

The response was a sigh so loud that it came with a burst of static. "Yes… The order told me to get her moved out of her house."

"They did?" I asked. That was good. It meant the order had it together enough to protect innocent humans from Melanie, even if it didn't care about an innocent vampire like Liana.

"Yes," said Roberto. "Our efforts have been a disaster."

I shut my eyes. "Please tell me you didn't go into her house veiled and try to influence her to take a vacation?"

Silence.

"No…" said Liana. She'd plucked her salad out of the bag of fast food and had stopped wrestling with the packet of dressing to scowl in the direction of my phone.

I motioned for her to give the dressing to me and tore it open at the corner before handing it back. "You did check my notes about Cassie before you went into her house, right?" I said to Roberto.

"There were no notes. Everything from your time here in Taos was expunged from our database."

Expunged? Because they didn't agree with how I'd handled the situation with Liana? Or from malware Darissa had left behind? We were still battling that, too. I made myself unclench my jaw. There were only so many burgers I could eat right now to take the edge off my constant hunger. Stress only made me hungrier.

I switched my phone to speaker mode and set it down on the console between me and Liana, putting a finger to my lips to tell her to stay quiet.

She drizzled dressing over her salad and began stabbing at the leaves with her fork, harder than necessary.

"Cassie has obsessive compulsive disorder," I explained. "She's always fighting the voices in her head demanding that she do certain things, and she manages her condition by finding ways to ignore them. Trying to talk her into doing something while invisible is the worst thing you could do, literally. She'll just do the opposite."

"Yeah, well… What should I do, then? I got Lydia to go over and talk to her, but Cassie just threw her out."

Liana looked like she wanted to speak. A speared piece of lettuce was hanging off her fork, forgotten halfway to her mouth.

"Okay, hang on," I said. "Liana, you got any advice?"

"If you already made her feel like little voices were telling her to leave, and then you sent a person in to say the same thing," said Liana, "you're going to freak her out. No wonder she's not answering her phone." She crammed the salad into her mouth and crunched away.

"In other words, we don't know what to do because all the logical options have been foreclosed upon," I explained.

"I can't watch over her constantly."

"Yeah," I said, "Liana and I will figure something out. Thanks for taking my call."

"Of course. Let me know if there's anything I can do."

I hit the button to hang up and turned to Liana. "You got any ideas?"

Rather than respond, she frowned, took my phone, opened the door, and put it on the ground outside. After she shut the door, she turned back to me. "I'm probably overreacting, and I know your phone is different from mine, but why are you so confident that we can call people on it and talk about my aunt's situation without being eavesdropped on?"

"Our phones are way more advanced than anything on the market," I explained.

She nodded, but didn't open her car door. "Okay, but who's to say the companies who produce that tech aren't owned by Melanie? Or Darissa? Or whatever the third one's named?"

"Because… I don't know." A creeping dread came upon me. "I trust the people who've told me our cell phones are fine. The president has a secure cell phone."

"First of all," said Liana, "no he doesn't. Second of all, even if it was secure from human terrorists, that doesn't make it secure from ancient vampires. The Nabateans are older than you."

"People can't eavesdrop on my kind, and vampires definitely can't."

"Yeah, but when you're talking to a non-angel, or when someone like me uses your phone, that's a different matter, isn't it?"

No… I thought. My order talked to humans on cell phones all the time. Surely the Nabatean sisters couldn't have been listening in on all those conversations? We weren't that stupid, were we?

"Also," she dug in, "a cell phone is pretty easy to turn into a remote bug. Maybe vamps can't spy on you that way, but they may be able to overhear me."

"No," I said. "No way…"

"And if you're talking to me, or interacting with me, then anyone else in the car would be able to see you do that. Does that mean your conversation on the phone could be eavesdropped on?"

This was making my head hurt. "I don't know."

"How did Melanie find me so fast after blowing up my house?"

"We didn't discuss going to the beach house on a cell phone. I think she followed your car. Siobhan was all confident that the neighborhood was clear, but these days?" I shrugged. "Cameras can be tiny and they could be hidden anywhere."

"And how would she follow my car?" she asked.

"I dunno. She could have looked up the beach house's location once she saw your lawyer. Or put a tracker on your car somehow…" I shut my eyes and put a hand to my forehead.

"So there could be a tracker on this car too," Liana pointed out. "This car was out of our sight for the whole time that you and I were climbing through the sewers."

"Storm drain."

"I couldn't smell the difference."

I looked down at my empty burger wrapper and although I was still starving, I also felt a little sick. "If she's using trackers, then yes… she could have put one on this car. We should probably ditch it just to be safe." I moved to get out but she put a hand on my arm, only to remove it like the moment of contact had burned her. It hadn't; she hadn't touched my skin.

"What's the plan, then?" she asked. "We can't just ditch the car here."

"You see how fast she's moving. She wants you dead."

To her credit, Liana didn't look angry with me, even though the order might have screwed up badly. She just looked scared. "Can't we use it to mislead her? I mean… how about we drive it to the airport and leave it there?"

"How is that a mislead?"

"Well, I'm not getting on a plane," she said, as if this was obvious. "I'm going to Taos to take care of my aunt. I say we take this car to the airport after my friends have taken off, to protect them a little."

"Um…" I rubbed my temples. "Back up. You are going to Turkey."

"No I'm not."

"Liana—"

"My aunt is an innocent person," she said. "I may not be the super ancient being that you are with all your accumulated wisdom, but I'm pretty sure the reason I've kept my soul this long is because I choose to do the right thing whenever I can. Killing Darissa was the right thing, and I didn't lose my soul for that. Not right away. You were able to bring me back. Helping my aunt is the right thing, too."

"Doing the right thing may help you keep your soul," I said, "but it does not protect you from vampires. Especially not if the right thing is also the predictable thing."

Even before she began to speak, I knew what she would say, and that she'd be right. "We're talking about my soul," she said. "There are worse fates than getting killed by a vampire! I'm not leaving my aunt, okay? It's not going to happen. And I'm not trusting your order to help her because look at what they've done already."

"Okay," I said, "I need to do the right thing, too, and that may mean dragging you kicking and screaming to Turkey while I dispatch other people to protect your aunt."

"I don't trust anyone else. Do you? After that phone conversation you just had?"

"If you think you're smarter than an ancient order of angels," I said, leaning in.

She looked me straight in the eye, challenging me to finish that sentence.

Why was I bullying her? Time for honesty. "You probably are... Okay..."

Both of her eyebrows shot up. "What?"

"Let me call Siobhan and miscue her."

"I'm not *that* brilliant, Corban."

"Give me my phone back."

NINE

"Code fourteen," I said into the phone once Siobhan had picked up.

"Fourteen?" She was indignant.

"Amber protocol."

She huffed, but nevertheless said, "Fine. God speed." That last she uttered in ancient Gaelic, her idea of a joke. Also a shining beacon to anyone eavesdropping that she was an ancient being. Then again, no one should have been eavesdropping. Our veils ought to have still worked.

Liana glared at me from the passenger seat, and also appeared to be taking off her clothes. She had her shirt hiked up.

I averted my eyes.

"Phone," she said, once I'd hung up.

I held out the phone without looking.

"If you have a code, why don't you speak in it whenever you're on a cell phone?" she demanded.

Ah, so that was why she was angry. I motioned for her to put the phone outside.

"I have it in a Faraday bag."

I looked back over at her and saw that she had pulled her shirt down and was holding up a small, black bag.

"You have a Faraday bag in your moneybelt?"

"I put my passport in it because it blocks RFID, but I realized it would also work for phones, assuming Melanie doesn't have a technology—"

"Stop," I said. "She's smart, she's old. Let's not drive ourselves insane thinking of all the advantages she might have using technologies that might theoretically be possible."

"Like invisible drones that could be parked overhead at the moment, ready to take us out?" asked Liana.

"Or the ability to create a simulation that feels like reality that she uses to torture us while our brains are actually in a jar in her lab," I said. "There's being cautious and then there's being pointless. Do we know of any kind of information carrying waves that can penetrate that?" I pointed to the black bag.

Liana shook her head.

"Then we assume that works, and that she knows that we're worried about your aunt in Taos because you said so over the phone."

"But she doesn't know that we think the car is being tracked," said Liana. "We didn't do anything to search for a tracker."

"Should we?" I asked.

"No, come on. How hard is it to just put on two trackers or three? Assuming people will stop looking when they find one? Besides, you can put trackers all kinds of random places."

"See, you really are the brains in this operation," I said.

"Okay, why do you keep saying stuff like that?"

"It's only the second time."

"Corban… You say I'm smarter than your order. Explain, please."

It was a mistake to tell Liana about the order's weaknesses. She'd be dangerous enough as it was if she ever turned fully vamp. I couldn't lie to her, though. "The order's still recovering from Darissa," I said. "That's why we're still short on scientists and researchers and people to reconstruct the archives of the artifacts we have. That's why Amy was able to help us so much. We got knocked back hard. I mean, that's war, right? We're not the super ancient organization with massive accumulated wisdom that we could be. Things have been a mess for centuries."

"Oh."

"So… yes, while we rebuild, maybe we are making dumb mistakes like not realizing that our phones aren't secure. Maybe we shouldn't blindly trust the company who makes them to be on the cutting edge. We're used to being invisible." I picked up my burger wrapper and dumped it back in the bag the fast food had come in.

Liana watched me. "Does making me invisible take up that much energy?" she asked.

"No… I'm dealing with some other stuff. It's a conversation for another time."

Her posture was uneasy, awkward even.

"I'm fine," I assured her. "Let's get this car to the airport and get another car."

IT MADE THE most sense for us to walk from the airport parking lot to the rental car joint. I put my arm around Liana's shoulders. She slipped her arm around my waist. I told myself this was because we had farther to walk and it was easier to sync our steps that way, but I hoped no one from the order spotted us.

We rented the car with a false identity that I had on hand for emergencies and paid for it with a credit card in that name. The manager of the rental car place was having a seriously bad day, releasing a steady stream of espresso-like hate until I tried to sip at it and she locked herself down. It was a typical human reaction. People walled their minds when they sensed themselves being messed with.

I was losing my edge. I used to be able to gently drain away suffering so that the person didn't feel what I was doing until they realized that the world was a brighter place.

Once I signed the rental contract and got the keys, we were on our way towards New York City in a white Nissan. The late afternoon sun slanted in through the windows and Liana asked me to stop at a gas station so that she could buy some sunglasses. The place I found reeked of spilled fuel, hot asphalt, and crushing boredom, and I could tell it grated on Liana to have me walk with her like I was her boyfriend. Even for a short jaunt like this.

I didn't do a full arm-around this time.

Still, she grabbed the first pair of sunglasses she saw on the rack, paid for them, and then we headed back out of the convenience store with the jangle of the bell mounted on the door.

"Are you going to tell me what Code Fourteen is?" she asked as she climbed back into the car, stubby nails clawing at the price label on her plastic tortoiseshell shades. She might have had the vampire prettiness, but she didn't do the typical vampire manicure routine.

I waited to answer until I'd climbed into the driver's seat. "Well… I can tell you how I'd translate it from ancient Gaelic."

Liana stopped picking at the price sticker and looked at me.

"Code Fourteen meant get to safety and don't wait for me. The Amber Protocol meant whoever was talking was about to go undercover for a while. A while for us could be a few decades or longer… but I don't plan to stay off the radar that long."

"Siobhan's an ancient Gaelic warrior?" Liana's tone was sarcastic.

"Yeah."

"She is?"

I nodded. "One of the most brilliant generals of her time. She just died too young to make the history books. The fact that she let Melanie get this close to killing you twice looks bad, I get that, but if it's a fight between Siobhan and anyone else, even a Nabatean vampire? My money's on Siobhan. And when it comes to protecting your friends? There's nobody better. I've known Siobhan for almost six hundred years. She only sounds like a modern Irishwoman because she keeps her accent up to date. We all do."

"Okay. Fine. Can we stop somewhere that I can get a pillow and a book next?"

I started the car. "Yes but let's put some miles between us and…" It occurred to me to be careful with how I phrased the next lines. Liana was coping with the loss of her house and the exile of her friends by distracting herself. I needed to help her with that and not bring these things up callously. "…Melanie's crew," I finished.

"Fine." Her clipped words indicated the silent treatment was about to start again.

I pulled the car out onto the road and headed for the freeway, narrowly missing a blue hatchback that cut us off. The person inside spewed aggression like boiled honey. I stifled the urge to scarf it all down and focused on driving instead. Sipping at his rage only made me hungrier. Not good.

You're helping Liana run for her life, I reminded myself. Of course you're burning through your reserves.

Liana began to fidget.

I did my best to not let this new distraction stress me out more. "Everything okay?"

"Can we just talk about the elephant in the room?"

That felt like a poke in the chest. I didn't want to have that conversation, but I owed it to her. She was mortal. I couldn't put things off with her.

I opened my mouth to say yes.

"We're being followed," she said, twisting around in her seat.

I glanced in the rearview mirror and saw that we were, indeed, being followed by a girl who looked too young to drive. She was behind the wheel of a Chevy Suburban and had dark hair but tawny eyebrows. A bad dye job to cover up something only an immortal would know to look for.

TEN

"She's fine," I said.

"You know her?"

I glanced in the rearview mirror again. "Well, not exactly."

"But she's fine? What do you mean? She's not a contract killer?"

"Just, first of all, was she the elephant in the room?" If she was, I would feel like an idiot.

"No…"

"Okay. Sorry, I wasn't sure." Though I had the impression I should have been, and that I'd just scored another demerit.

At least Liana didn't rub it in. She stuck to her line of questioning. "She's not a contract killer… how do you know that?"

"I know her type. I'm pretty sure."

"What do you mean you're pretty sure?"

"I'm... I would be very, very shocked if she hurt us, and at my age, it takes a lot to shock me. It doesn't bother me that she's behind us. It's actually kind of interesting."

"Interesting how?"

"I can't really tell you anything about her because that's the deal she has with my kind," I confessed. "She reveals as much as she wants, to whomever she wants and if she finds anyone spreading information about her? She disappears. I'm not being coy, okay? Her kind are just very secretive."

"Should we talk to her?" Liana asked.

"We let her make all the moves."

"But she's following us. That's a move, right?"

"All the moves," I repeated. "She won't hint. She'll just do."

"And you can't tell me anything about her?"

"Sorry," I said.

"Can she read minds? Would she know and get you in trouble? What if you told me and I promised to play dumb?"

"I'm pretty sure she can't read minds," I said. "But please let me honor the covenants I've made. I'm not hiding anything that would hurt you."

That had the desired effect. Liana looked away, chastened. "Are there supernaturals who can read minds?"

"Maybe."

"I did not need to know that."

"I agree," I said. "But you asked. I'm not sure that mind-reading supernaturals are any more dangerous than really good guessers or really intuitive people, though."

Liana nodded. I could see from how she fidgeted that she was doing her best not to return to the topic of the girl behind us, even though curiosity burned in her.

I, meanwhile, did my best to cut my mind loose from our follower. It was always a risk, scaring one of her kind off or invoking their… wrath wasn't the right word. They didn't do cruel things. They just disappeared and never showed up again. They blacklisted individual angels all the time. Ours was the most delicate of truces, and the fact that I'd sustained mine for as long as I had made me extra-keen to keep it. Even though the timing of her appearance made me extremely curious.

"Maybe we should talk about this elephant?" I suggested. Nothing would take my mind off our follower like having my heart smashed with a sledgehammer. My heart didn't beat, but it sure could ache. First, though, I owed Liana another apology. "I'm sorry about laughing at you—"

"You're fine."

"Not if I ever made you feel like I trivialized your feelings."

"No, you made me feel like you have a really weird sense of humor."

"Well… okay. I guess that's fine. It's accurate."

Liana began to pick at her nails. "I told you that I never got over you."

And I never got over you, I thought. "I'm sorry if that's made your life difficult."

I pressed my fingertips against the steering wheel, checking to see how hard I had to press for my nails to make contact.

Liana zeroed in on this. "Why do you do that?"

I glanced to make sure that I understood what she was asking about. "I don't like my nails getting too long. It's harder to climb and stuff if they are."

She lifted her gaze to my face. "Oh. I thought maybe you played an instrument or something."

"No. I refuse to play the harp. Sorry if you got your hopes up."

"I totally did."

"Even in ancient Ireland, when it was a perfectly manly thing to do, I never played the harp," I said. *No*, I thought, *stop joking around with her*. How was it that we'd only spent one week together and yet she could trade quips with me better than Siobhan? If we were going to discuss this elephant in the room, I needed to shoot that elephant dead.

Okay, bad analogy...

"Listen," I said, "I need to explain something to you."

She stopped picking at her nails.

"What happened... what I did to save you, it can't happen again." The memory of my lips on hers surfaced up in my thoughts and my hands began to tremble. I tightened my grip on the steering wheel.

"Right."

"And I don't mean because I don't want to or anything like that. It's literally not possible for me to do." Did she hear the catch in my breath? I hoped not.

"So did I hurt you?"

"No," I said firmly. "You didn't." I had hurt myself. Liana was blameless.

For a moment she turned her back on me and looked out her passenger window. The only sounds were the whoosh of the air conditioner and the soft rumble of our tires on asphalt. My gaze was forward, but I could see her silhouette in my peripheral vision as if it were a great black hole, yanking on my attention.

With a sound that might have been a sob, but was too soft for me to tell, she turned back towards me. "Can I ask if you did it just to save my life?"

"Yeah, of course I did it to save your life. If you mean to ask whether I minded having to kiss you to do it, no I did not mind that one bit." I had relived that kiss a million times in my dreams.

"Do you think I should have moved on by now?"

An entirely valid question. It cut like a knife to the chest. "I'm not going to judge your personal decisions. I think you should feel free to, if you want."

When her only response was the gaze of those deep, brown eyes, I added, "I do care about you. I can't be—"

"I'm not that arrogant." Liana laughed. "You saying stuff like that, it helps."

Her mind remained, even now, stubbornly closed off. Not once in all the insanity today, had she let slip even the slightest whiff or taste of what she felt. I could feel more from the bored drivers on either side of us than I could feel from her.

"It helps how?" I asked.

"Helps me get over you. I'm not trying to imagine you turning me down. You're here, actually doing it."

"Liana—"

"And it's what I need. So thank you."

Ouch. And yet, what was I supposed to do? This was good. It was right.

Liana deserved to be loved. Everyone did, but her especially. She wasn't mine and never would be. I was admiring the wife of a better man. A mortal man who could grow old with her.

She glanced at me. "I always knew, deep down, that you didn't pine for me." More laughter, an arpeggio of mirth that was like being struck up the side of the head with a mallet.

"And I know you don't really pine after me," I said, pushing back. "I'm not that great. I did ghost you, after all."

"On the orders of a divine consortium of angels," she pointed out.

"Which isn't perfect either."

"Okaaaay…" said Liana. "Why? Because they didn't ward off Darissa's attack?"

"No, that's not what I was thinking about. Never mind. I'm just… I guess I'm tired."

"You want me to drive?"

I shook my head. My hands were still steady on the wheel and the world was in focus. I wasn't sleepy, just mentally tapped out.

"I know the order was right to separate us," she said. "Knowing I wasn't over you, it makes sense. Not that I'm complaining about having you back. I just… I'm trying to say that I see the wisdom in what they did."

"Yeah, I wasn't actually thinking about that," I said. "I think they did the right thing with us, too. You didn't deserve to have your life be so weird."

Liana fell silent again, twisted to look behind us, then said, "She's gone."

"Maybe we'll see her again, maybe we won't."

"Thanks, by the way."

"For?" I asked.

"Being cool. Being nice about my human weakness."

"I am trying to be charitable," I agreed. "But it's hard not to judge you for your poor taste in men."

"Very funny." The words fell flat, though. She sensed I wasn't joking.

Or, that was my best read of a woman who still remained blank to me.

She chewed the inside of her cheek and averted her gaze out her window.

"Tell me how you've been?" I asked, desperate to fill the silence. "You've stayed friends with Gina and Amy."

"They're kind of my only friends, still," she said. "Ever since finding out I was a vampire and what that really means, I haven't wanted to make any new ones."

"Sorry to hear that."

"You once told me, when I asked how many other kinds of supernaturals there are, that the answer was part of a much longer conversation."

She did have a keen memory.

"Can we have that longer conversation?" she asked.

"I'm not sure it'll make you feel any less alone."

"But can we talk about this? I barely understand the world I belong to."

I worked each shoulder forward, then back, keeping the muscles loose. "Okay," I said. "I guess so."

ELEVEN

Liana kicked off her shoes and pulled her legs up under her, her body angled towards me. Traffic was still light, but was picking up steadily as we headed towards the Big Apple. The sun was starting to sink towards the horizon, and I hoped that Siobhan had gotten Amy and Gina out of the country by now. With my phone in that Faraday bag, there was no way for me to get any updates. I needed to decide when a good time would be to take it out and get more information. Was Siobhan worried about us? Did the order think we'd gone rogue?

"So," said Liana, "what's the most common kind of supernatural?"

"My kind," I said. "Angels. Even after Darissa's attack, there are still plenty of us, and new ones ascending all the time."

"Okay, that does make me feel less lonely. I mean, I know other members of the order don't necessarily like to talk to me, but it's good to know that they're everywhere. Second most common?"

"It depends. The thing is, vampires spread the fastest. They're virulent. Usually we're just hunting down a few ancient ones who are really smart, but every now and then one of them launches an attack and they can wipe out a lot of people really fast. In your lifetime, vampires haven't been very numerous."

"Got it. So what's the next most common kind of supernatural after vampires during an outbreak?"

I considered that a moment, then realized the answer was obvious. "Magic users."

"What? Like witches and stuff?"

"Fae, Sidhe," I said. "People can't just learn magic; they either have the ability or not. I mean… people with the ability have to learn how to use it, but you couldn't pick up a grimoire and just start casting spells, no matter how hard you studied."

"How common are we talking here? One percent of the population? Ten?"

"I have no idea," I confessed. "Sometimes I see them, sometimes I don't. I just see them more often than I see any other type. Your roommate in college was one."

"I knew it! Except… why didn't anyone tell me?"

"Why didn't you tell her you were a vampire?" I challenged.

"Right… I just might have felt less alone."

"Nobody likes vampires, and you might have gotten drawn into a whole lot of magical politics. Be grateful." It had been hard to believe a lone magic user picking Liana as a roommate was a coincidence, but the order hadn't found evidence of anything more than that.

"But if I see my roommate again—"

"You probably won't," I said. "Nobody from your class ever will."

Liana sat up straighter. "Did something happen to her?"

"She didn't die if that's what you mean. She's from an… enclave." That was the easiest way to describe it. "They often send their children to top universities in the US or Britain, but then they go back to their enclave and they don't otherwise interact with the rest of us."

"Oh…"

"It's nothing personal."

"That explains why she would never tell me where she was from. Is it like a cult? Are they in a compound somewhere?"

"Cults," I pointed out, "don't send their members to schools where they'll mix with the general population. The inability to have any meaningful interaction with others is what makes a cult a cult. They're groups you can't reason with. They'll just say you're lying or tricking them. Her enclave isn't like that at all. As for how they live? I've never seen it in person. They're Sidhe." (I wondered if she'd recognize the word; it was pronounced "Shee".)

"Which… aren't those, like, Irish fairies?"

Apparently she did.

"Technically," I said, "they're the mounds that fairy folk were believed to live in. But you know the Irish idea of a fairy isn't Tinkerbell."

"No, fairies are evil, right? Not that I'm saying my roommate is."

"They're their own people. They've got their own goals and philosophies. Sometimes they've done awful things, but not for hundreds of years." They hadn't done much other than keep to themselves for hundreds of years, then one had chosen Liana as a roommate.

But Liana didn't know that was strange. "That why you were in Ireland with Siobhan?" she asked. "Fighting Sidhe?"

"Fighting vampires," I explained. "A few Sidhe were our allies in that."

"Did you know my roommate's ancestors, then?"

"No idea." I shrugged.

"How long do Sidhe live?"

"Well… according to legend they age very slowly and live for centuries, but the actual people are a little more complicated. Suffice it to say, your roommate looked her age. Her kind have a way of… playing with time?" This was getting very hard to explain. "Your granddaughter might see her seventy years from now and she might look the age you are now, or you might run into her a week from now and not know who she is because she could be a stooped old lady."

"Playing with time?"

There was no way to talk around the truth of all this. It was best to be honest. "Supernatural humans are from other worlds," I said. "Think Narnia. In fact, I suspect C.S. Lewis knew more than he let on."

Liana, to her credit, didn't laugh or roll her eyes. She nodded, though her brows were drawn together. "Um, so they're not human?"

"They're human. If one of them shows up in the emergency room or the morgue, which happens, nobody's going to find anything amiss. Please don't ask me hard questions about which world humanity originates from. I'm not sure. My beliefs say it's this one."

"Are other worlds other planets or other versions of Earth or what?"

"I don't know. Being able to cross over is a really, really rare skill. It's not like there's much data about these other places. I think even among the Sidhe, only a small minority of them can come here."

"But if you're ascended, you're supernatural. Does that mean you're from another world?"

"Angels and demons are different," I said. "For one thing, we don't inherit our supernatural powers. We're part of Earth's creation. All other supernaturals in this world originate in other worlds, or are descended from people who crossed over. The ones who cross over and back, like your roommate, are unusual."

I watched Liana nod as she took this in. "Do magic users affect our world in any major, secret ways?"

That was the million dollar question, wasn't it? I shared the only truth I knew. "They are trying to combat climate change."

"They are?"

"They aren't having much more success than you mundanes, though."

"They call us mundanes?"

I nodded. "It's not meant as an insult. Not usually, at least."

"Okay… what's the third largest group? Werewolves?"

"I don't know." I shrugged. "And it depends on what you mean by werewolf."

"Huh?"

I laughed. "So, most human cultures have some kind of legend of people who turn into the apex predator of their region. Assuming those are true, there are a few different ways the shapeshifting happens."

"Like skinwalking?"

"Right. Though if you're talking about the Native American kind of skinwalking… the thing about Native Americans is that they've got the lowest percentage of altered humans by far. I'm not saying their supernatural beliefs aren't real, but they aren't…" I tried to think of the right word.

"Literal?" Liana suggested. "What you and I would consider literal?"

"Yeah, that's a really good way of putting it."

"One of my best friends is a Native American and an anthropologist, you know?"

"Honestly, I have *never* met a supernatural Native," I said. "That doesn't mean I haven't met ones with powers that are outside your world view, but that's different."

"Amy's a ferrum worker."

"That's not a supernatural thing the same way as being Sidhe or a werewolf is."

"Humph." She held up her hands and looked at her rings. "You sure ferrum isn't just iron from the world where vampires come from?"

"There's no vampire world. Vampires are demon-possessed mundanes."

"Well, ferrum workers must've crossed over from somewhere if they're supernatural, so why couldn't they have brought ferrum with them? They'd be from the same world, right?" She resumed staring at her rings.

I blinked at that. "Ferrum is a sacred metal," I said. "Ferrum workers are probably people from Earth given a divine gift."

"I'm religious too, Corban. Doesn't mean there isn't also a more scientific explanation of how these things work."

"You consider people crossing over from other worlds with magical powers scientific?" I asked.

"Hey, you're the one saying my worldview limits what I understand. If there really are other worlds and these inter-world mechanics, science can study that. And it seems like a possible explanation for—"

"You're making my head hurt," I admitted. She had a knack for doing that.

"Sorry." She turned away from me. After some time, she leaned her head back and shut her eyes.

Why did her mind have to be so nimble? Now she had me questioning everything about the origin of vampires and angels. But was that new? I'd been questioning everything ever since I'd seen her kill Darissa, and then come back from damnation.

When she remained quiet, it was clear our conversation was over. She was probably dozing, and that left me with only my memories to fill the silence.

TWELVE

Four years ago and one week after we first met, Liana had sacrificed her soul to kill Darissa. She had to use a vampire power to do it, so she let herself turn completely, giving her body over to the demon inside her. I was just around the corner when it happened, but by the time I got through the door, Darissa was dust and Liana lay on the floor, dead. Humanly dead, at least.

This happened in the little mountain hamlet of Taos Ski Valley, in an urgent care center that Darissa planned to use to run tests on Liana. It was nighttime, and I'd been one step behind the whole evening. That's why I was too late to intervene before Liana executed her insane plan. Her insane plan that had worked.

Darissa was dead and Liana would have risen as a vampire in hours, and it was my job to stop that. Her vampire self would have all her memories, and likely her intelligence as well. She'd be worse than Darissa.

Logic, virtue, benevolence, my covenants, all of these dictated that I had to end Liana then and there.

I couldn't do it. I'd fallen to my knees beside her, looked on her pale, bloodless face, cool tears welling up in my eyes. She'd made me promise to kill her if she turned vampire, though. I owed that much to her. I couldn't bring myself to cut her throat or stab her heart, but I could ensure that she faced sunrise one last time a few hours from that moment. That would burn her to ash.

But I didn't want to see Liana Linacre become ash. I wanted her alive again. I wanted this strange, powerful girl back.

Being a man of faith, I prayed deeply and desperately for the Lord to give me some guidance, not that I expected any. That's when the impression came to me that if I held her underwater, perhaps that would quench the flames and leave her body intact. It gave new meaning to the concept of baptism by water and fire. I didn't see how that saved her soul, but in that moment, I was going to try whatever idea took root.

Her body was far too light when I carried her out to the car. She didn't breath a single breath for the entire, half-hour drive to Cassie's house.

Cassie had answered her door with a scowl, but one look at her niece caused her features to shift.

"I might be able to save her," I said. "But you have to invite us in. I know she told you not to." This wasn't fair to Cassie at all, but I chose her house for a reason. It was an Earthship, which meant it had a water cistern. Hers was set in the floor of her downstairs studio and would get some of the first rays of sunrise.

Cassie didn't hesitate. "Corban, Liana, come on in, guys."

To Cassie's eye, Liana would have looked like a corpse. I suppose she was. She still didn't breathe as I submerged her in the cistern. In the hours until sunrise, I knelt and prayed and meditated. Cassie sat on the stairs, watching me. It was the sort of night that passed so slowly that my memories of it seemed to encompass lifetimes, and not the sort that swept past in the blink of an eye—lifetimes where I was in the moment, feeling the crawl of years.

Yet the sunrise did come, first with the intense lightening of the horizon and the clouds catching the pink and peach hues. Liana lay still at the bottom of the pool, and its surface was constantly rippling thanks to the indoor waterfall that splashed down into it, so I couldn't make out her features clearly. She did not seem to be getting bloated or waterlogged.

Such were the dismal thoughts I felt standing on the lip of the pool, staring down into it as the room got lighter and lighter.

When the sun peeked over the horizon, I climbed into the pool and lifted Liana high enough that she would catch its rays, filtered through the water. Her body was light yet solid, her skin still smooth and intact. The moment the first dapples of sunlight hit her, she began to move, which startled me, and she began to float, as if there was still air in her lungs.

She kicked and began to struggle. I held her firmly down, watching to make sure her legs didn't break the surface. The water began to heat rapidly, steam rising up in a great curtain that drenched me and condensed in fat droplets on the back wall, and still Liana struggled, though when her eyes popped open, I sensed a shift in her movements. No longer was she trying to break the surface or get away. She was just trying to feel where she was and what was going on.

That's when the water began to boil with large bubbles bursting at the surface and still more steam flooding the room. I had a hand on her breastbone, holding her down, and felt her movements get fainter and weaker. She was letting herself be restrained, and she was losing strength.

That's when I knew that Liana, my Liana, was fighting for control of her body. Her soul hadn't left after all, but her body was weakening. I had to save her, so I dunked myself underwater, held her close, and placed my lips on hers.

My intention was to heal her, of course, but there was an element of carnal pleasure as well, even though I'd never kissed anyone and didn't know what I was doing. Even now I could remember the feel of her mouth warming against mine, and the leap in my chest when her arms went around me and her fingers ran through my hair. The second kiss was easier, and the third felt completely natural as I relaxed into it.

Her mortal soul reclaimed full control of her body in a great pulse that instantly cooled the water around us, saving her from some rather devastating burns, no doubt. She clawed her way to the surface and started breathing again, I think. I blacked out.

My kind are too pure to touch tainted flesh. We can endure some casual touches to heal humans who are sick or injured. An intimate touch, like a kiss, though, is far more dangerous. To touch such thin skin to the equally thin skin of a tainted mortal overwhelms my kind.

But the next thing I knew, I was being hefted out of the pool and onto the concrete floor. Liana even managed to cradle my head so that I didn't crack it against the cement. I'd coughed up the water in my lungs and it slowly hit me that the pounding feeling in my chest wasn't just waterlogging, but rather something else I hadn't felt in millennia. My heart was beating. Blood was moving through my body.

I reached out to touch Liana's hand and she pulled back, to protect me from the expected pain.

"It doesn't hurt," I told her. I put my hand on hers again, and I might have repeated that it didn't hurt. I don't remember. The world went black after that.

When I came to, I was among my own kind, only they weren't my kind anymore. They had me laid out on an exam table in a nearby hospital and were checking my vital signs, exchanging looks of horror and confusion as they did. Michael Esai, an old friend of mine who'd been a doctor in his mortal life, and two other angels were there. They agreed that I had simply lost my powers. It happened to our kind in very, very rare occasions when we did too much healing. The order flew me to Turkey, and there sat me before a tribunal, mainly so that they could gawk at me, I think.

Nobody really addressed the obvious issue, though. They took what had happened as a miracle, I suppose, or at least a divine action they weren't going to question. Though I questioned it all the time.

They did opt to keep me away from Liana, of course. It made no sense to let a two thousand year old guy stay with an eighteen year old girl. She was to live out her mortal life, having been pulled back from the pit of hell by her own discipline and the kiss of an angel.

I'd spoken to her one last time on the phone, and heard the anguish in her voice. She missed me, and I missed her. In that moment I'd relished the mournful feeling, the sadness that clung to me like a sopping, cold blanket. It was supposed to be temporary, after all. I'd assumed that I was a tourist in mortality given another human moment, like a bonus chapter of a favorite novel, twenty centuries after my mortal life had ended the first time.

Over time, my powers did return. My body cooled, and my heart stilled. Human flesh became tainted to me once more as my body purified. Michael's diagnosis had been correct.

But during my time as a mortal, even though I knew better, I'd flirted with damnation. With mortality and a human body came human desires, and it was my misfortune to have ascended while in my late teens, or perhaps early twenties. I was a red-blooded male once more. Women were desirable again. Constantly.

My best distraction were those memories of touching Liana's hand without pain, or the feel of kissing her. This one would slip into my consciousness as I drifted off to sleep or first thing in the morning. I suspect the sin had already been committed, but my ruminations after the fact did not help. Like a fool, I'd let these feelings linger with me. I let myself wish, like the weak mortal I was at the time, that I had held her hand for longer, that I had kissed her again.

I ached to hear her voice, her laugh. I spent far too much time even in what I thought were innocent memories of eating burgers with her in Taos. But it was during one of those meals that I'd confessed to her that she was more than a friend to me. When I was at my weakest, such as late at night, I dreamed she was there, lying with me.

She was beyond my reach, so what was the harm of dreaming? I thought that I was safe even by New Testament standards because I wasn't affecting her in any way and I wasn't betraying anyone else. Nevertheless, what happened next is entirely my fault.

When my powers returned, they came with dark impulses to hurt people. That's when I had to examine my motives for pining after Liana.

What I felt was love, but it wasn't the pure love of my kind. I desired her, wanted to have her for myself, wanted to annihilate anyone else who might look twice at her.

And now that I had my powers back, I could fall. I could abuse my powers and unleash a constant stream of pain and suffering on humanity. I could collapse an empire the size of Rome by myself.

Now, as I drove across Pennsylvania and into Ohio with Liana sitting in the passenger seat beside me, it was both easier and more difficult to fight the darkness. It was easier because having her here was an effective distraction. My thoughts of running a school bus full of children off the road so that I could saturate the air with delectable terror were easy to ignore when

I could instead focus on the sound of her breathing and the way she shifted in the seat.

It was harder because my destruction sat beside me. She was temptation incarnate. One slip and I knew I'd have my arms around her again, throwing caution to the wind, and bringing damnation down on both of us.

If she sensed any of these dark thoughts on the drive, she gave no sign. I watched the hours crawl past and the sun set and the clock turn to the wee hours before deciding to stop at a small motel in Ohio. "Get some sleep here," I told a groggy Liana as I parked the car. "I want to time our entry into Taos to coincide with the *touristas* flooding in."

She rubbed her eyes, stretched, and waited for me to escort her from the car to the front desk of the hotel. I don't think she noticed the creature who lay crouched in the brush, just beyond the end of the paved parking lot. The watcher's eyes glowed, but softly. I felt a thrill as I returned the gaze.

THIRTEEN

O nce Liana had the amulets set out in the four corners of her cheap but serviceable hotel room, I left her. I didn't need to be around while she changed into the nightshirt she'd bought during our stop at a superstore, or to watch her step out of the bathroom in a cloud of steam with her hair wet and glistening.

Besides, I wanted to see if that watcher was still lurking around the parking lot. To my dismay, there was no sign of her, which dashed any hopes that she wanted to talk to me.

Perhaps she was just stalking Liana.

I did a quick circuit of the hotel and paused to sip the pain of someone battling nightmares. If I had to guess, it was someone who'd been in combat and couldn't leave the horrors of the battlefield behind.

When I turned away from their door, I found myself face to face with another of my kind, an elderly woman with wispy, white hair and ramrod straight posture. "Do I know you?" she asked.

"I'm just passing through," I said.

She didn't ask for my name, which I was grateful for, and I didn't ask for hers. She took up the post by the sufferer's room while I took a better look around. That meant scaling the side of the hotel—its brick and mortar walls rough against my hands—leaping over to a nearby streetlamp and grabbing its metal girth, then shimmying up it so that I could look out across the flat town. Its cluster of lights was sandwiched between cultivated fields, velvety-dark after sundown. The light post was a precarious perch, but I'd clung to worse with a lot more at stake than needing to get a look around.

My strength and reflexes weren't supernatural. I had to train like a human to hone them. Two thousand years ago, I'd kept myself busy during quiet nights by doing my combat drills, adapting my style to suit a dagger rather than a gladius, but that gets boring after a few hundred years. I'd branched out into other forms of hand-to-hand combat. Those centuries had been so *long*, though, or seemed that way when compared with the modern era and its exercise fads. In decades I'd gone from tired old routines with only slow, gradual modifications, to thousands of new styles available on YouTube. My latest obsession—for the past decade or two—had been Parkour. While the world slept or my services weren't otherwise needed, I ran and climbed, my heart singing at how much I could vary my routine based on the buildings around me. Tonight my exertions were wearing me out, though. I climbed back down the lamp post and returned to the hotel.

The lights were out in Liana's room, but I still coughed politely before opening her door—its lock slid open at my touch. Inside, Liana rolled over in bed to look at me. She wasn't asleep, and that wasn't good.

"Sorry," I whispered. "Did I wake you up?"

"No… I can't sleep."

She had ample reasons for that. Memories of her house would probably consume her for years. I was glad we'd gotten out of town without her seeing the charred husk of the place, but she would likely regret that. She might be angry with herself for not being the one to go through the wreckage for keepsakes and valuables. Siobhan and Liana's lawyer would coordinate that effort and anything that could be saved, would be. But Liana, being Liana, would still wonder and blame herself for all the things that could not be saved.

Worry for her friends was likely another concern.

She didn't need me barging in, traipsing around her room at night as if this were normal or the kind of thing any girl would find acceptable.

Then again, barging in and then fleeing wasn't great either. If I was here, I should at least do my job. I walked over to the bed and looked down at her. "You want some help before sunrise?" I held out a hand.

She looked at it uneasily, then looked me in the eye.

I didn't react. This had to be her decision. I certainly couldn't let my desire to touch her be a factor.

After a pregnant pause, she began to reach for my hand.

"Can you take your rings off?" I asked.

She blinked and looked at me, but slipped the ferrum rings off without comment before holding her hand out. I think she expected me to press the palm of my hand against the back of hers, using her thicker skin to shield me somewhat.

I took her hand in mine so that we were palm to palm, and the pain that shot up my arm wasn't as bad as I'd feared. She might still have vampirism in her system, but it was very, very mild. I hadn't cured her of the condition with that kiss, but I'd definitely knocked it back. I'd also healed enough humans in the last four years to be well accustomed to the burn.

She refused to look me in the eye as I held her hand, waiting for the last of her vampirism to dissipate. I expected to feel a surge of hunger then, but I didn't. Just the usual burning desire to go find some pain to gorge on.

When I let her hand go, she slipped her rings back on, whispered, "Thanks," and turned over in her bed so that her back was to me. I don't know if she slept, but I suddenly felt tired. I caught an hour or so (according to the clock on the nightstand) of sleep in one of the chairs by the window, then went to take a shower before she woke up.

SOMEONE WAS WAITING for me when I stepped out of the bathroom. Someone I hadn't seen for a very long time.

He was much shorter than me, coming up to about the middle of my chest. His skin was the dark shade one would associate with sub-Saharan Africa, but his eyes had the epicanthal folds one would associate with east Asia. He was watching Liana sleep with a critical eye. She was clearly restless.

When I stepped into the room, he motioned for me to follow him outside, where the air was still warm, despite the absence of the sun for so many hours. The humidity held onto the heat. The horizon was lightening but it wasn't quite sunrise yet.

My friend turned to face me and held out a hand in greeting. He always did the modern thing, which meant a handshake this time. It was in keeping with his modern mode of dress, which today meant jeans and a t-shirt, and his habit of speaking whatever modern language was used wherever he was.

"Otuo," I said. "Is that still your name?"

"I'm happy enough to answer to it."

"How'd you find us?"

"I had help. From a friend."

I wanted to ask if the girl in the Suburban was the friend, but if she wasn't, she would not be happy about me revealing her presence, so I held my tongue.

"I've brought some of Liana's things," he explained. "Her clothes, from her car."

"How'd you get those?" I asked.

"Siobhan. Or, one of her teams, to be precise. They took possession of the vehicle and managed to get the intruders out of her lawyer's house. Only some minor ransacking. He'll have it open again as a vacation rental tomorrow."

"Liana will be happy to know that."

Otuo looked me over. "How do you fare?"

That phrasing sent a chill through me.

My old friend smiled, unconcerned that his cover as my tribunal was blown.

I shrugged. "I'm hungry a lot. I slept a little last night. But I'm still here, am I not?"

"And how's Liana?"

"Well, I think. Not much vampirism in her system that I can tell."

"And how are you and Liana?" he pressed.

I lifted my shoulders. "I'm her guardian, her friend. Nothing more. As you said."

"That's what she wants?"

Why was he pushing this point? "It's what's best for her."

"I see. Your precaution of destroying your cell phone was… interesting."

And probably looked terrible, like I'd gone rogue and kidnapped her. I didn't bother to explain that it wasn't destroyed, just masked. "Sorry," I said. "Liana thought Melanie might have tech that would enable her to eavesdrop on us."

"That's unlikely. Our phones have state of the art security."

"Then how do you know I destroyed my phone?"

He lifted his chin slightly and didn't answer. "May I ask what your plans are?"

"The predictable plan," I said. "We're going to help Cassie. It's what Liana feels she has to do."

"That is most predictable, yes."

"Are Amy and Gina safe?"

"They are. Siobhan set up a false lead with one flight and put them on another. The false lead was delayed by several mechanical failures. By the time Melanie's minions had finished searching the plane, Siobhan and the girls were halfway to Turkey."

"Excellent."

The hotel room door opened and Liana leaned out. "My friends are okay?" She'd gotten dressed while we spoke.

"Eavesdropping?" I accused her, then did a quick scan to make sure there were no other locations that might conceal other eavesdroppers. I stepped out into the parking lot to survey the roof.

"Your friends are fine, yes," said Otuo. "I've got a duffel bag full of your clothes and some other things to give you, and then I'll let you two be on your way."

The roof was clear. Just plain gray asphalt shingles.

Liana shut the door behind her and followed Otuo across the parking lot. We were able to transfer her things in short order. Then we said our goodbyes, Liana cleared her things out of the hotel room, and we climbed into our rental car to drive to a nearby diner for breakfast.

When we turned onto the main road, a familiar, beat-up Suburban pulled out to follow us.

FOURTEEN

The girl didn't approach us as we pulled into the diner parking lot, only stood by her car and watched as we went inside. Liana noticed her, of course.

"We still wait for her to make all the moves?" she asked me.

I nodded, though I shared her disappointment. I wanted to talk to this mysterious stranger and find out what she wanted.

The diner looked like something straight out of a fifties television show, complete with a metal counter and a woman in an apron pouring coffee for the patrons. I snagged a booth in the back corner, a location from which I could watch the whole room. The place smelled like frying bacon and eggs and the windows were dusty, softening the morning light to a golden hue.

Our follower was nowhere to be seen while Liana and I ordered our breakfasts—waffles for her, just coffee for me. There was a lot of anxiety in this agricultural town, so I sipped away on that also. The girl didn't poke her head in until the server had gone back into the kitchen, and then all she did was make a beeline for the bathroom.

To anyone else watching, she would appear to be a rootless drifter, using facilities and grabbing food however she could. That's the impression Liana got too because she couldn't sit still any longer. "I'm going to go see if she needs money or anything."

Habit told me to stop her. One never approached one of this girl's kind. Then again, it was more in keeping with preserving the girl's anonymity if I let Liana treat her like any other human. Liana seemed mildly surprised that I didn't escort her to the bathroom. I stayed put while she pushed her way in the door.

The girl emerged a moment later, stuffing what looked like money into her pocket and not sparing a glance in my direction. Liana emerged a short time later and looked out the front windows.

I turned to see what had her interest, and caught sight of a skinny coyote darting from behind the Suburban and off across the empty lot next to the diner, headed for a nearby McDonald's. If I'd had a beating heart, it would have begun pounding right now. As it was, I felt only deafening silence as I turned back to Liana, who was slipping into her seat.

"She's a were-coyote?" she asked in as low a voice as she could manage.

"Shifter," I said. "She's a coyote-shifter, and it's very, very rare for them to reveal themselves to anyone."

"So you knew that's what she was?"

I shook my head. "I suspected that's what she was, but you never really know unless they do what she just did. And now that she's shown you, we can talk about her, but you don't talk about her with anyone else, ever, okay? Not even another member of my own kind."

"Well, if shifters are a thing, what's the big secret?"

"I have no idea," I confessed. "Did you talk to her at all?"

"No. I just asked her if she needed anything, and the way she looked at me? I'm not sure she speaks English. She wouldn't take money out of my hand, so I left it on the side of the sink and went into a stall. The money was gone when I came out."

"Yeah, she got it," I said. "I saw her put it in her pocket."

"Good." Liana nodded, satisfied. "So why would this type of shifter be so... shifty?"

I chuckled. "The only other things I know about coyote-shifters are that they're very rare, pretty much always operate solo, and they're associated with elevated numbers of supernaturals."

"Huh?"

"Wherever you see one operating? There's usually a group of some kind of supernaturals nearby. I don't know what kind of relationship they have with other supernaturals, though. Anyone who talks too much about their kind gets shunned by all coyote-shifters."

"How many of those have you seen?" Liana asked. "Shifters like her?"

"Not many." I couldn't be more specific than that. I couldn't list the one who'd been a friend of mine five hundred years ago, or the one who'd always pranked me three hundred years ago. "So, the way to spot them is that they have unusual coloring.

Like dark skin and naturally blond hair or light skin and purple eyes. But they can easily dye their hair to blend in."

"If they shift into coyotes, they're just here in the US, right? Or, North America, I guess."

I shrugged. "I can't answer that." I had seen them in North Africa and Europe and had run into them many, many times before I ever saw a regular coyote. It had been jarring to come to North America and see what I assumed were packs of supernaturals running around all over the place. Not until I saw a hunter kill one did I figure out that there were plain, non-shifter coyotes in the world.

"But Native Americans don't have a lot of altered humans?" Liana asked.

I shook my head. "No hot Native werewolf guys nearby. Sorry."

Liana spluttered a laugh at that and we both stopped talking as the server came with our coffee and Liana's waffles, which smelled like crisped batter with a hint of nutmeg.

As Liana began to dig into her food, she said, "I was totally hoping to be swept off my feet by a Native werewolf."

"I know." I quelled the usual surge of jealousy; it was clear she was kidding.

"Have him imprint on me and all that. Be devoted to me for the rest of his life."

"Hey," I said. "That's real."

"It is?" She blinked and paused in her chewing.

"Yeah. When they bond with someone, they really do bond for life."

"Huh. Okay, I won't joke about that. They must usually marry other werewolves, then."

Again I shrugged. "These people aren't common, so it may not even be possible for them to marry their own kind. They usually marry regular humans. The kids have roughly a fifty percent chance of inheriting the condition." I took a swig of my coffee, and Liana watched me swallow, unasked questions lurking in the depths of those dark brown eyes.

"I guess I'm still not fully recovered," I said. "From four years ago."

She nodded. "I'm sorry—"

I held up my hand. "No apologizing. I'm okay, you know?" Yes, I felt like I was starving most of the time, but working in refugee camps reminded me that a lot of people starved in this world. It wasn't the most comfortable existence, but it was manageable. I couldn't seriously look at my lot, at the long life I'd had and the experiences I'd accumulated, and say my suffering was "unfair." There were countless people who had it a lot worse than I did. Despite my hunger, I felt pretty put together this morning. Talking to Liana grounded me.

"So who was your friend who came by this morning?" she asked. "What was his name? Otuo?"

"Yeah. He's one of the oldest members of the order; I'm not even sure what his age is. He was old when I ascended. Rumor has it that he's the oldest living angel."

"Wow. I was kind of wondering if he was, like, a really ancient form of human. The way he looks…"

"I have no idea. I've seen him a lot and talked to him a lot, but I don't know much about him. He was always my superior. When I ascended, he managed the order in what you now call Africa. Back then that meant he travelled all the time, keeping caught up on new members and making sure we were settling in all right. I'd see him every few years when he did his rounds through Syria or what you now call Algeria. That and the rest of the Mediterranean used to be my territory."

"How'd you end up here? In the US?"

"I followed fair skinned people. Which isn't strictly necessary because few people see me as it is, but it's a good precaution. I ministered to people on a ship bound for Massachusetts Bay Colony and spent time there for a couple hundred years, then went west. The climate in New Mexico is close enough to northern Africa, it was comfortable."

"Massachusetts Bay Colony?"

"Yeah, had my last run in with Melanie there, actually. She ran a brothel in Boston and Siobhan and I figured out she was a vampire. Siobhan and I came over on the same ship."

"Right," said Liana.

Was I imagining it, or was she acting a little hurt? Was she jealous? Of Siobhan? Siobhan was beautiful, all right, but I'd sooner kiss a goat (and I may have been an ancient Greek, but I wasn't *that* kind of ancient Greek.)

Liana was back to eating her breakfast with her usual, detached demeanor.

After a few more bites, she looked up. "So what happened when you figured out what Melanie was?"

"We got a gang together to raid the brothel. We didn't know how old Melanie was, or that she'd been sighted previously. Again, back in those days, it wasn't easy to keep coordinated records. People would journal what they saw and send those journals to the Citadel, where archivists would file and cross reference things, but it wasn't like we could call the Citadel for a briefing or anything."

"You guys used to mail your journal entries all the way to Turkey?"

"Courier," I said. "Regional supervisors would do their rounds and then report in at the Citadel every few years, with all the journals of everyone in their region. I mean, sometimes they got mailed. Like, if the person wrote in a language nobody along the route would understand, then it was safe to mail them. But then the Citadel asked us to always write in the modern language of the time because we couldn't count on there being archivists who could read obscure dialects that died out hundreds of years ago."

Liana was drinking this all in, like the nerd that she was.

"Anyway," I said, "when we went to raid the brothel, we took precautions, but we didn't realize we were dealing with a vamp that had been around long enough to have some tricks up her sleeve. She booby trapped the doorway. That doesn't always work on my kind, but it worked this time. We only made it partway into the building before she started clearing everyone out."

"What, like all the brothel workers?"

"Yeah."

"Why would she want to protect them?"

"So… I don't know," I said. "What we did figure out from raiding the building was that the brothel was a front for a lab of some kind. She appeared to be breeding humans to get certain characteristics. Like, she'd spent years trying to get eyes a particular shade of blue, for example. I don't know what that was about. She'd turn the people, then kill them. It followed no pattern we could make sense of."

"Huh…"

"But here's the main point. After we raided her lab, she killed all of her test subjects, all of their children, everyone who'd worked at the brothel, all of the johns that had visited, all of the beggars and street urchins who'd ever loitered in front of it, the police officers that patrolled that neighborhood—"

"What, like in this mass slaughter?"

"No," I said. "That would have drawn too much attention. She got a lot of people with an outbreak of cholera, and then she picked off the rest over the course of decades. She also expunged all reference to the brothel in all the city and county records. That block looks like it wasn't even built up during the time that she ran it, and she burned the brothel to the ground and expunged all records of that fire."

"You're telling me that she's ruthless and thorough," said Liana.

"Yeah. And very cold and detached about it, not a hothead like Darissa was."

Liana nodded. "What else should I know about her?"

"That she's impossible to know. She could have pulled off a hundred other deletions of data like that since then. She covers her tracks."

"Right… And there's a third sister?"

"Who may be dead."

Liana blinked.

"She hasn't been sighted for centuries," I said, "and about the time she disappeared, Melanie and Darissa tried to take us down again. They were not happy with whatever happened." I shrugged. My kind hoped that a rogue angel had ended Gamlat. That was back at a time when our membership records weren't perfect, so we didn't know who it was. One never trusted the Nabatean vampires to be dead, though, unless we'd seen them poof to dust with our own eyes.

"What was the third sister's name?"

"Gamlat. She kept the Nabatean name and was the most Nabatean of the three."

"Like, how?"

"Always stayed near Petra," I said. "Always seemed a lot different, more traditional than her little sisters. She seemed to be a lot older than them, and may have been a half-sister or something. That wasn't uncommon back then. She had darker skin, coarser hair, and was the absolute boss. The two younger ones practically worshipped her."

Liana opened her mouth to ask another question, but was cut off by the sound of screeching tires and crunching metal on the street outside. Everyone's attention swung to the two cars that had collided. One was on its side.

What Liana and the others couldn't see, though, was the intoxicating, delicious waves of pain that rolled off the scene. My hunger screamed, demanding that I pounce. I was out of my seat and to the door before I was even aware I'd moved.

FIFTEEN

"Corban," said Liana, her voice faint and in the distance.

I was already out the door of the diner, headed for the accident. A large gray pickup truck had hit a little Honda Civic—one of the old models, which was tiny with thin walls that had buckled in deep folds on impact. Whoever was in the driver's seat was about to bleed out. I could sense their life blood pouring away as their consciousness shrieked in wordless pain.

Other cars had stopped and used their blinking hazard lights to make a barricade, the drivers and passengers spilling out onto the road, cell phones in hand.

Whoever was in the pickup truck appeared to be all right. I could read that from the reactions of onlookers as easily as I could taste their fear and pain wafting towards me. The driver was injured, but not seriously.

Those who approached the Honda all recoiled and backed away. One woman put a hand over the eyes of her teenage son, who rounded on her in annoyance.

A hand closed around my arm and dragged on me to stop.

Liana, her eyes squinting in the sunlight, her face pale. She didn't speak, only looked into my eyes to try to discern what I was thinking.

Well, I wasn't. I was starving and there was a buffet of steaming hot suffering that I had to get to. I shook her off and resumed walking towards the wreck, dimly aware from the sound of shoes striking asphalt that Liana was keeping pace with me.

This might be gory, and I wondered if I should try to get Liana to stand aside. This was Liana, though. She wouldn't take orders from me, and she did have a degree in biology. Maybe she could take it.

The Honda lay with its roof facing the diner, its side (which now faced the sky) caved in. I was able to leap atop the wreck with a standing jump, and land lightly on the mangled remains of the door with its few shards of glass remaining in the window. The windshield had stayed intact, though it had gone white with a myriad of tiny fractures.

From this close, I could smell the familiar scent of blood and gore, the sweet copper reek of death.

But the driver was still alive, and looked up at me with eyes wide and fearful. He could see me because he was not long for this world, but from this angle he wasn't too badly maimed.

His shirt was soaked with blood and a vein had burst in his left eye, dying the white a dark red. I wanted nothing more than to absorb all of his pain, all of his suffering, and revel in it.

That way, I knew, lay disaster. His pain wouldn't slake my thirst, it'd only enliven it. That being said, I was already starting to absorb it. I was like dry ground and him a geyser of water. What hit me was going to sink in; that was how the laws of the universe worked.

I needed to stop his pain, and I needed to stop it fast, or else I'd go from being starving to ravenous. I knelt down and put my hand on his bare arm. He stared at me, uncomprehending.

Then the healing kicked in. I felt the man's body start to knit, the gushing blood slackened off as new flesh stopped its flow.

If I got in our rental car and drove it onto the freeway, a little voice in my mind said, then slammed on the brakes to create a pileup, I could reap pain as rich as this in greater quantities. Intellectually I knew it was wrong, but I was tired of being hungry. I'd fall at some point. Why did I fight so hard to put it off?

"Corban?" Liana was scrabbling up onto the car, moving with impressive athleticism.

"Stay back," I ordered her.

But this was Liana. She got on top of the car and peered down into the driver's seat. Just then, the burst vessel in the driver's eye healed and the reddened sclera went white again. My healing had penetrated deep enough that even the broken bones were beginning to straighten. He was going to live.

Despite this, I couldn't release him. My fingers wouldn't open. My fear that any more pain from him would push me over the edge kept me healing him, heedless of how it sapped my strength. This would only make me hungrier. The sensible thing to do would be to let go, but still I gripped his arm.

People had started to notice us and were beginning to assemble around the car. Not good, not good at all. My veil was down.

A figure pushed through from the back, the gray haired angel I'd run into last night. "What are you doing?" she demanded, leaping up onto the car.

She paused to blink when she saw Liana react, but then she turned to me. "Let him go. He's healed."

I couldn't, though.

The man's eyes rolled back and his body began to seize.

The woman reached for me but I gave her a look that froze her in place.

"You'll kill him," she said.

But the man wasn't dying. His body was going slack, yes, and his pain and other emotions were clearing up, but he wasn't about to expire. He was ascending. His heart slowed and stopped and his skin began to glow. He gasped in a deep breath, then another as the last dregs of his pain evaporated.

When he opened his eyes again, they were the most improbable shade of silver, almost metallic.

The other angel looked at me with respect. "Sorry," she said. "I didn't know."

She hadn't known this man was a candidate for ascension. Neither had I. She thought I'd perceived the man's worth and come to help him join the heavenly host. I hadn't. I'd merely pressed my hand to a spurting font of emotion, desperate to make it stop.

"The tamer of demons shall set them free," the man said, in a language so obscure that it would sound like gobbledygook to anyone who overheard it. "And the moon has risen over the starlight kingdom."

I released my grip on him and nearly fell off the car, I was so weak and dizzy.

"I'll take care of this man," the gray haired angel said. "You, girl. You need to help this one feed on some emotions. Some pain. Some fear. He needs to recover after helping someone ascend."

"No," I whispered to Liana. "I can't."

"Get down off the car," she said to me between clenched teeth. "I'll get you some food."

I half slid, half dropped to the asphalt below and Liana landed next to me. Touching only the cloth of my sleeve, she wrapped my arm around her shoulders and her arm around my waist; this was a familiar routine.

Rather than take me back to the diner, she hauled me over to the McDonald's, where she ordered me a Big Mac and some fries.

I sat down to eat just as the ambulance pulled up outside. Had this entire process happened that quickly? I took a big bite out of my burger, reveling in the greasy taste of the meat and the bite of pickle and mustard. I washed it down with mouthfuls of what turned out to be water in my soda cup.

Liana was watching me from across the table with narrowed eyes. "You okay?"

I nodded but didn't look at her. I would be okay. I would. I was clawing back control. The fear and anxiety that rolled off the accident scene outside was now no worse than the usual anxiety that permeated a refugee camp. This, I was practiced at warding off, but still it pressed at me. Still I wanted to run out and gulp down the pain and suffering and fear.

"Corban." Liana leaned into my line of sight.

You can't hurt her, said the voice in my mind. I wouldn't, ever. The thought of her suffering in any way made me want to weep, and with a few deep breaths, I felt my hunger's claws release from me. It was still there, still raging, still demanding that I feed it, but I could look away.

I might not be the man Liana remembered, but I wanted to be as much like him as I could. The look of fear she gave me made me sick.

I ate more of my burger, swallowed, and said, "Thanks." One syllable was all I could manage, so I held up the burger as well.

"Corban, what's going on with you?"

I took a few more deep breaths. The red haze was fading from my vision. "That was a lot of pain," I managed to say, with my mouth full. "It was intense."

"That guy, I'm guessing, wasn't on your list to ascend. Or does God send you people like that, victims of car accidents whose past you know nothing about? Does it just happen that people who survive your healing process ascend?"

"Treating strangers in car accidents is not usually how it's done," I conceded.

Liana already knew that, though. She was barely listening to me. "I mean, that other angel, she was freaked out with what you were doing."

"I'm sorry about that."

"And why are you eating so much food? Here, do you need another burger?"

"I might," I confessed.

Liana slid out of her seat and went back up to the front.

I polished off my burger and fries and drank the rest of my water, then went to refill my cup with Coke. I didn't have a regular human body. Junk food didn't seem to hurt me in any way, and if I had to eat, I might as well enjoy the experience. To me, modern junk food was the nectar of the gods. It was probably a sign that I was tragically lacking in class and refinement, but I didn't care. The machine age had brought with it processed food in improbable colors and textures, and I loved it. (Except for Pop Tarts. Those were a bridge too far for me.)

Liana returned to the table at nearly the same moment I did and pushed a tray with another burger and more fries towards me.

I was able to thank her this time before ripping the wrapper off and digging in.

She watched me like a disapproving babysitter.

I wiped my mouth. What was I supposed to tell her about what was "going on" with me? I didn't fully understand it myself.

"Can I ask something else?" she wanted to know.

I nodded.

"The tamer of demons will set them free?"

It wasn't just jarring that she repeated the words, or that she repeated them in the language they'd been spoken in. I nearly choked when she repeated them again in English.

"What does that mean?" Her gaze bored into mine.

"It's… how could you understand that?"

"Yeah, well, I was going to ask that too, but first, what does it mean?"

"It's an old prophecy, about the devil," I said. "He formed the armies of fallen angels in heaven and they were set free when they were banished to hell."

"That's not freedom," Liana pointed out.

"Well, the English isn't a perfect translation, I guess."

"I didn't hear it in English."

"Look, I dunno," I said. "It's what I've always been told. Everyone who ascends repeats the prophecy, and we know it was fulfilled when Satan unleashed the host of hell. I mean, the way they torment humanity on Earth shows they are free to do that, right?"

"Okay, a couple of questions," said Liana.

I nodded and sipped more Coke. Lucky for me, the restaurant was pretty dead at this hour. The only other patrons were a couple of teenage guys at the far end of the room, reading off their phone screens. There was no sign at all of coyote-girl.

"First…" Liana held up one finger. "Is there a literal Satan and his minions running lose on Earth right now?"

"I don't know if there's a literal guy named Satan," I said. "But I think so. And yeah, there are fallen angels that torment people. Along with demons like the one trying to possess you."

Liana nodded and held up two fingers. "You sure that prophecy isn't about me?"

SIXTEEN

"Y-yeah," I said, but she saw my hesitation so I quickly added. "It's not about you. It's been repeated by everyone who's ascended for-for as long as people have been ascending."

"How do you know that? I've tamed my vampire demon, haven't I?"

"Be-cause… that's what I've always heard." I took another bite of burger, this time hoping to forestall more questions.

"And the moon has risen in the starlight kingdom? What starlight kingdom? Where?"

I shrugged. Not only did I have no idea, I did not want to talk about that part of the prophecy. The first part that she'd recited was ancient. The second part I heard for the first time when I healed a kid too aggressively soon after I got my full powers back. He'd uttered the two parts of the prophecy and confused the heck out of me. Later, another member of the order explained that every angel was reciting it when they ascended, and sure enough, everyone I'd seen ascend since had uttered that second part along with the first.

I wasn't a master theologian. I didn't know offhand what the starlight kingdom was, and there was considerable debate on the subject. I had faith there was an answer, though. Truly, I did.

Liana was looking at me with her lips pursed and her eyes narrowed again. Boy was I getting tired of that look. It was the same look she'd given me when we first met. Well, not right when we first met. The first look she'd given me was abject terror, which faded to suspicion when I made it clear I wasn't going to kill her.

I needed to get my mind to calm down. Thoughts were bouncing around inside me like ping pong balls in a bingo shuffler.

Liana had shifted her gaze to something out the window, and when I looked to see what it was, I almost choked. The gray haired angel and the newly ascended guy were headed straight for us.

"We have to get out of here," I said.

"We do?"

"Now!"

"Corban."

But I was already gathering up my food in my arms.

Liana, being Liana, cleared up my tray and trash, which we did not have time for. I headed for the exit at the far end of the dining room, hoping she would keep up with me.

I also hoped the teenagers reading their phones wouldn't take note of us, though that was probably wishful thinking. Did

I really expect them to ignore a young couple tearing out of the place like we were wanted for a crime? Or perhaps my veil was restoring itself.

Once outside, I pressed my back to the building and took a good look around. Aside from traffic on the road (which moved slowly thanks to the accident) and a farmer in the distance driving a tractor, the coast was clear. I went swiftly around the building until I had line of sight on our car in the diner parking lot. With another look around, I headed for it.

I didn't hear Liana's swishing through the grass until I was halfway across the empty field. "Why are we running from your kind?" she asked, her voice conversational. I wondered if she'd been working out, or if the vampirism made her so fit.

"I don't want to talk to them."

"Do you want help carrying your food?"

Yeah… I looked pretty ridiculous striding across a field with a half unwrapped burger, carton of fries, and soft drink cradled in my arms. "No," I said.

"But the order is cool with you being here with me? We're not running from someone who'd want to separate us?"

"No," I said.

"I am confused, okay? I'm going along with this, but you are definitely confusing me."

"Sorry," I muttered. It was only a few more strides to the car. "Um… can you drive? Keys are in my pocket." Was that skeezy of me to ask her to get my keys out of my pocket?

She fished them out with a tolerant shake of the head and unlocked the car. "You can't just unlock it?" she asked.

"No." I could open a locked car, but it wouldn't unlock. Once I shut the door again, no one else would be able to open it.

Once we were both inside, with our seatbelts on, she turned to ask me a question, but I shook my head. "Drive."

"Yeah, this is totally how I expected things to go with an angel protector," she muttered as she started the car and threw it into reverse. But despite her disdain, she followed the example I'd just set by driving it around the back of the diner onto a small access road and then taking a roundabout way back to the main thoroughfare that the diner, hotel, and car accident had been on.

I finished my burger and fries before then and was sipping at my soda as we turned back onto the smooth asphalt and headed for the freeway.

"Can I ask what's going on now?"

I expected Liana to be angry, but when she looked at me, her eyes were dancing with amusement.

"Um…"

She burst out laughing. "This makes no sense, okay? Explain, already."

"Your trust in me is disturbing."

"Yeah, well deal with it. You went against your order to protect me and saved my life once, so I do trust you. And it's not like I ever thought you were normal."

"I'm… too tired to talk right now."

"Fine."

Little did she know that I wanted her to drive because the thought of causing a traffic pileup wouldn't stop playing on my mind. It was on repeat as I tried to puzzle out how I could survive it and gorge myself on the terror I caused.

I was pretty sure I could prevent myself from actually doing it. Liana's safety, for example, would have been at risk, but I still fantasized about it, which meant I did not deserve the smiles Liana kept flashing my direction.

I had enough anger with myself that I was able to turn my back on her, channeling my best teenager moodiness.

"Um, Corban, where do I go from here?"

"You get on the freeway and stay on it until Colorado."

"Oh."

I settled myself against the seat and shut my eyes. Even if I couldn't sleep, I could get some rest.

I WOKE UP with a start to the same view of flat fields of corn that I'd last seen in Ohio, but the clock on the dashboard said I'd been asleep for two hours.

At my sheepish glance, Liana gave me a slightly worried look. "You okay? You need more food?"

"No, and yeah, I feel better now." The dark mood wasn't gone, nor was the hunger, but they were both manageable.

"So are you going to tell me what's going on with you or not? And let me make something clear, if you decide you can't tell me, I'll trust your judgment."

These were kind words, but she flung them at me like a dagger. Dang her. She knew exactly what to say for maximum impact. How could she know me so well after so little time?

"Fine," I said. "I'll tell you." Now I just had to decide how much truth to tell.

SEVENTEEN

I couldn't outright lie to Liana, and I knew that any partial lie I told would eat at me too. I was in the position I was because I hadn't adhered fully to the covenants I'd made, and honesty was one of those covenants. Whatever I told her, I had to ensure that it didn't put me in an even worse position.

Liana remained patient, flexing her hands one at a time before placing them back on the wheel. The highway was relatively empty, and thus there wasn't a whole lot of free floating emotion. Even those cars that were near enough for me to feel the emotions of the occupants seemed to be driven by contented people. Either that or people who had their minds locked down, like Liana.

"I'm not supposed to be alive," I began.

She glanced at me, but stayed focused on the road.

"Kissing a human is fatal to my kind."

"What, always?"

"Always before now."

Liana's mouth twitched, with annoyance or fury, I couldn't tell. "Why would you risk death for me?"

"Because you're a good person. And I know life isn't fair and bad things happen to good people all the time, but when one of my kind is in a position to create a just outcome, that's our responsibility."

"There are better people than me who die every day. In your entire life, you must've seen thousands of them get killed."

"Okay, I don't want to get in some long argument about this," I said. "The thing is, what you've done with your vampirism is unprecedented."

"So you've never seen someone like me get turned before. I mean, if you look at things statistically—"

"Hey," I said. "Don't get nerdy on me, all right? You wanted me to explain what's going on with me? Let me do that without you shooting down my motives and stuff."

"Right. Sorry." She bit her lip. "About you surviving, is that maybe because I'm not human?"

"Kissing a vampire definitely means death for my kind. There have been vampires in the past who've enjoyed killing my kind with kisses and other... more intimate stuff."

Liana shot me another brief glance, too quick for me to read anything from it.

"Anyway," I said, "ever since I got my powers back, I've been really unstable. I can't stop thinking about hurting people and creating big orgies of pain. I'm not well..."

"That's terrible. I'm really sorry if I did that to you."

"This is not your fault."

"If I hadn't let Evan—"

"Stop," I ordered her. "Or if you have to blame someone, blame Evan for turning you. That was his choice."

Liana pursed her lips, thinking. "So you turning evil would be you falling, right? That's how it works?"

"Yeah."

"I'm really sorry."

"You ever felt this way?" I asked.

"Not long term. Sounds like you're dealing with this long term. That night when I almost bit Pedro and had to run off, yeah. I could taste his blood and knew exactly how I wanted to bite him and how long he'd live before I sucked him dry. I can't imagine feeling like that all the time."

My shoulders lifted. Many people talked about feeling a weight they didn't know they'd been carrying being taken away, but that's not what this was. I'd known full well the weight I carried. It just never occurred to me I could ever share it with anyone. Members of the order did not talk about the darker side of what we were, and anyone who knew how I struggled would regard me with suspicion. They'd be right to.

But Liana carried a stigma of her own. There were no good vampires, despite how many modern entertainers tried to create them. Vampires were blood-sucking demons, and their immortality meant they didn't value human life. People were food, and were insignificant. Even a vampire who behaved by most of society's rules was still a sociopath, and since they could do what they wanted without being penalized for it, they always did sooner or later. Everyone, especially my kind, hated vampires.

"Is your life ever not a nightmare?" Liana asked.

"What's happened has been rough, yeah. It's been painful, but it's also been amazing. I mean, that's life, right? I don't like starving all the time, and I don't like fantasizing these awful things, but I also didn't know I could do it until I had to."

"I've known people who deal with ideation before," she said.

"Which is?"

"When you think about or plan out awful things. Like people who plan their own suicides."

"Oh… right." I was aware of the phenomenon, or more exactly, I had fed on plenty of guilt people felt from their dark daydreams. I wasn't sure if hearing that humanity had a name for it was reassuring or dispiriting.

"Did helping me last night make your situation worse?" she asked.

I considered that. "No."

"How about making that guy ascend?"

"No. It just made me really hungry."

She glanced at me.

After a moment, she asked, "What's that guy's family going to think? That he died in the car accident?"

"Most likely, yeah."

"Okay, so help me understand how that works."

"The reality that people see isn't actual reality," I said. "It's filtered. We all patch over things we don't understand, and my kind has an ability that boosts that process somehow. Most people believe their ascended loved one died. Sometimes they think they've gone away on a trip and then somehow forget to worry about when they'll return. As best as I can tell, it's like veiling. People's minds take the shortest path of least resistance to an explanation that keeps their reality making sense."

"Gee, Corban, that's *so* simple. No wonder you always talk about what a dummy you are."

"Compared to you, I am."

"No you're not." She shook her head. "So does anyone outside the order know your situation?"

"Just you."

"It seems like the kind of thing a vamp could use against you."

"Yeah… I know. I'm not sure how Melanie would know, though. Nobody in the order talks about it at all."

"And you're sure coyote girl wasn't working for Melanie? You're positive?"

"Coyote-shifters *hate* vampires," I said. "As in, like, will try to kill them every chance they get."

"Oh, and you let me go into the bathroom alone with her?"

"Well, look, if she saw you as a vampire, she would've attacked you last night while she was watching us check into the hotel. She was in coyote form, you had more vamipirism in your system, and she could've taken you down, no problem."

"Did the fact I was with you help?" Liana asked.

"I have no idea. There are members of her kind who know what I am, but I don't know how much they communicate with each other, and if they do, I don't know what their consensus would be about me. Sorry, it's a really mysterious group." I stretched my arms over my head.

Liana fell into an uncomfortable silence. She kept readjusting her grip on the steering wheel and wouldn't look at me.

"Okay," I said, "what?"

"There's something I should tell you."

"What's that?"

"I'm not sure if it means anything, but I get all the results of blood tests the order does on me."

"Yeah?"

"And I also have seen ones done on your kind."

"Right." I wasn't sure what she was getting at.

"They're the same."

"What do you mean, they're the same?"

She chewed her lip a moment, then said, "I mean angels and vampires have identical test results on all the modern tests. A biologist wouldn't be able to tell us apart. If they knew what to look for, which most won't."

"Weird," I said. "What do you think that means?"

"I don't know."

"Why don't you let me drive now?" I glanced at the time on the dashboard and then tried to get my bearings. It was impossible to know exactly how many hours we had left without using a phone GPS.

"We're in Illinois," said Liana.

"Okay, pull over the next chance you get and switch places with me."

She gave me an uncertain look.

I gave her my best, reassuring smile.

LIANA SLEPT FOR a lot of my shift behind the wheel, no doubt exhausted by all the crazy drama. Also, sleep in a car didn't count for much. People could do it for hours and still not feel rested, so I wasn't too shocked when she drifted from unconsciousness to severe lethargy and back again through the rest of the day and the following night.

That gave me plenty of time to stew about what she'd said about blood tests. Was my battle with falling really like her battle not to turn into a full vampire? I hadn't struggled like this before, though. Liana had struggled with becoming a vampire every day until I'd healed her.

My kind had the power to help and heal people. Vampires did not. My kind fed on emotion. Vampires sucked blood. My kind were virtually invisible to humans. Vampires had no reflections, but were otherwise perfectly visible at all times. Vampires couldn't endure sunlight. They shape-shifted into a mist form. They were entirely different creatures.

Except neither of us could touch ferrum, and we both understood the weird language of the prophecy.

There's an obvious answer to this, I told myself. We were different creatures with a common origin of some kind.

Yet my mind wouldn't settle on that. It couldn't find purchase there, because the longer I drove the more I wondered if a fallen angel was my true form. Was I, like that girl I'd cornered in the girls bathroom four years ago, keeping myself from being fully possessed? Maybe I was being ridden by a different kind of creature than the demons that made vampires vampires, but the feeling of fighting for possession of myself rang true in a deep and resonating way. That disturbed me.

It continued to disturb me as I finished the drive west and turned off the main road. I had to drive a lot of little back roads that took us around Taos after sunset because I wanted to approach the city from the direction that tourists driving from Santa Fe would take the following morning.

The beautiful high mountain vistas were shrouded in darkness; all I could see was the dirt road ahead, lit by my headlights. A herd of elk peered at us from the side of the road at one point, their eyes glowing dimly.

We pulled into Dixon—a little town near the road to Taos that was known for its crafts fair and apple orchards—at about five in the morning. Liana managed to wake up enough to blink her eyes and look at me. The horizon was awash with light and sunrise would happen soon.

I held out a hand to her. "Let me heal you, and then I need you to climb in the trunk."

Liana, being Liana, said, "Cool." She slipped her rings off and gripped my hand with hers, wincing at the pain, but sparing a tense smile for me regardless.

Then it was on to the last leg of our journey. I hoped, fervently, that Cassie was still all right, and that my order hadn't done anything else foolish. Without the use of my phone, I had no way to know for sure. Then again, I'd ministered for centuries without the benefit of a smart phone. Whatever awaited us, we would handle.

EIGHTEEN

After I drove through the city of Taos on the way to Cassie's home, I passed a weathered depression in the open desert, all that was left of the great crater Liana and I had created when we killed her sire, Evan. He'd gone into his vampiric mist form and had hidden in the maze of burrows created by some prairie dogs. We'd trapped him there and waited for his strength to give out, and when it did, he'd popped out of mist form and blown up the prairie dog town in the process. That was the one major drawback of mist form. It took a lot of energy to sustain.

I never did hear how the cleanup of the prairie dog town went. Cassie had handled it.

Her subdivision had a lot of open space between the houses, and this was high desert plain, so no trees or anything to obstruct the view. I could see Cassie's house from nearly a mile away, and there was nothing obviously wrong with it. Though from this distance, all I could discern was that it was there, and that there was no great column of smoke rising up from its general location.

That put it in better shape than Liana's childhood home.

I approached carefully, scanning my surroundings and praying that Liana was doing all right in the trunk. She had assured me that stories of people asphyxiating from carbon monoxide in car trunks were urban legends. The fact that she listed YouTube pranksters hiding people in car trunks as her evidence didn't entirely convince me. I decided instead to trust in the fact that she really was very smart.

The dirt road was rutted and uneven, and I did my best to drive smoothly. I didn't want her black and blue by the time we arrived.

At a quarter mile out, I could see that there were two cars parked in the driveway. One was Cassie's—not the same car that she'd had when I'd lived here, but one that screamed with her personality. It was a PT Cruiser painted an improbable shade of dusky pink.

The other was a minivan, which led me to assume many figures would be milling around near the house, but as I drove closer, I only saw one.

He stood, staring at my car, a hand shielding his eyes from the sun. His stance and his height gave him away. Otuo.

My old friend had come to look after Cassie.

As we rolled up in the driveway, he greeted us with a smile.

"You made it," he said, as I opened the car door and got out. Hot, dry air that smelled like sun-bleached grass and dust assaulted my senses. It felt good to be home.

"How's Cassie?" I headed around to pop the trunk.

"You see how he is?" said Otuo. "First thing he wants to know is how the mortal fares."

I looked up to see someone else getting out of the minivan. Mouse, who's real name was Inioluwa, but who everyone called Mouse because she was fiendishly good at sneaking around undetected.

"Cassie's fine," said Otuo. "No sign of vampiric activity in the area at all. No one probing this house. The coast seems clear."

Liana sat up stiffly as soon as she was able, slipping her sunglasses onto her rapidly blinking eyes. She hissed as the sun hit her skin, but endured it.

"My aunt is okay?" she asked, climbing out.

"Yes, aside from being agitated," said Otuo. "I sent Roberto away. He's doing his work in Taos. I took over here."

From this angle, the house looked a bit boxy, but not too unusual. It was, however, extremely unusual; all the houses in this subdivision were. Its outer walls were made of used tires and rammed earth and the interior walls were made out of empty bottles and concrete.

Liana smoothed her hair as she looked at her former home. "Have any of you talked to her?"

"No," said Otuo. "We've left her alone, just watched the house. If you could talk her into leaving, though, we have a good, safe place for her." He produced a brochure.

I didn't need to look to see where it was. There was a little spa retreat up north that was run by a member of the order, and which was favored by other members of the order. When angels felt overwhelmed, or burned out by their eternal existences, that was where they went. The brochures were exclusively used to get select humans to go there, but if they ever tried to find it again or recommend it to a friend, it would appear that the place had gone out of business. I'd helped the owner ascend over a century ago, as she was reaching the end of her life and distraught that her time serving others was going to come to a close.

"Okay," said Liana, scanning down the page. "I should be able to get her to go there."

Mouse stepped forward, quiet as her namesake, and Liana looked up at her, causing Mouse to freeze, surprised.

I hid a smile.

Mouse sketched a curtsey. "You really do see more than most," she said.

But Liana only shrugged, gave a polite greeting, then started towards the house while the rest of us moved instinctively towards the minivan. It was best if Cassie didn't see it and have cause to wonder.

The front door opened to Liana's knock and she slipped inside.

I turned to look over the Taos Valley once more, at the flat plain with the jagged canyon running through the middle distance and the mountains far enough to be tinged blue. The air at this altitude was ultraclear; one could see fifty miles or more. I'd lived here for decades, which wasn't actually all that long for one of my assignments. I'd been in Ireland for over two centuries, for example. Nevertheless, Taos had stayed with me. It was quirky and strange and the place where I'd met this one girl.

As soon as Liana disappeared into the house, I began to walk around the structure. The other angels followed suit. I could tell from Mouse's stance and carriage that she'd been working on her fighting reflexes, and they'd been remarkable to begin with. I had helped her ascend too, back in the day. She'd been Yoruba, and a soldier. I didn't remember if she'd had to hide her gender for that, or the details of the war, only that Mouse had slashed her way valiantly to protect some children caught in the crossfire, and received a killing blow in return. I'd managed to get her leather helmet off so that I could touch her skin with my hands, and there, on the battlefield, she'd become one of us.

The Earthship appeared secure. Through the south wall of windows I could see Cassie had been dying a lot of yarn lately. Her studio was a riot of color. At the back of that room, set into the floor, was the pool where I'd held Liana submerged that fateful morning.

Liana and her aunt came down the stairs, conferring with each other. Cassie had the brochure in one hand, but from the set of her mouth, it didn't look like the conversation was going well.

Although Liana kept her eyes on her aunt, with one hand she made a subtle wave, a sign for me to help her out.

I wasn't sure how to do that, but I went back around to the front door and knocked. It took a while for anyone to answer, since they were both downstairs, but when the door did open, it was Cassie who frowned out at me.

"Hi," I said, so that she'd see me.

Good old Cassie, with her hair up in three pigtails and a baggy dress that might literally have been made out of a gunny sack. Spindly legs, like those of a chicken, stuck out beneath the hem and her feet were encased in silk slippers.

Liana was climbing the stairs behind her.

"Corban's here," said Cassie.

"Yeah, I know." Liana came to stand in the middle of the kitchen, behind her aunt.

"I asked her how weird things might get if I didn't leave," Cassie explained to me. "She didn't answer, but then you knocked. This is my answer, isn't it?"

Cassie had made it clear that she did not want to believe in the supernatural, but seeing me revive Liana gave her little choice. In her heart of hearts, she knew neither Liana nor I was fully human.

"Yeah..." I said. "I'm sorry. But if you leave, you'll miss whatever weirdness that may or may not happen."

"And can I ask where you've been for four years?" Cassie demanded. "You kiss my poor niece and then disappear?"

"It's fine," said Liana. "We don't have to talk about that."

I wondered if Otuo or Mouse were within earshot, and decided not to look.

"We do," said Cassie. "What's your problem, treating her like that?"

"I almost died," I said. "And I'm not a legal resident of the US. Once I left for treatment, I couldn't come back."

Cassie snorted. "I wouldn't have let that get in *my* way."

"I'm sure you wouldn't."

"Liana deserves someone who wouldn't let it get in theirs. We clear?"

"Yeah," I said. "I agree."

At that she rolled her eyes. "Fine. I'm leaving. I'll go to that place in the brochure, as long as you can promise it isn't weird."

"It's not," I said. "It's a Zen Buddhist—"

"Buddhists are totally weird!" Cassie snapped. "You don't think they are?"

"I… don't have a strong opinion."

"They do good retreat centers," Liana offered. "They're a useful kind of weird."

"Well, that's true," said Cassie. "And Liana's going to be safe?"

I looked at Liana, which was the wrong move. Anything but an immediate nod was the wrong move.

Cassie put her hands on her hips.

Truth was my only way out. "Whoever killed your brother," I said, "is active again. That's why we want you to go somewhere safe, and somewhere hard to find."

"Was he killed by someone or something weird?"

"Unfortunately, yes."

She flung up her hands. "Fine. Now I feel guilty for running away."

"Aunt Cassie," said Liana. "Let me look after you for once. You always said you didn't want to be the responsible adult. Well, I do."

"That is not how I meant… You know what? Fine." Cassie turned around and headed for the stairs. "I'll get packed up and I'll go and are you staying here?"

"No," said Liana. "But the people at the retreat will know the best way to contact me." She didn't bother to say that the best way might be no way. That was a problem for later.

I pulled the door shut and turned around to find the other two angels had watched the entire exchange. Otuo had his arms folded across his chest and a satisfied smile on his face. "Well, at least something's gone right."

"That doesn't sound good," I replied.

Mouse gave him a challenging look and he rolled his eyes. "After this," he said, "come up to the Ski Valley."

"The Ski Valley?" I asked. "What for?"

"Liana can talk to Amy and Gina from there," he said. "And you and I need to talk as well. The order's in grave danger and it's well past time that you joined the inner circle."

"I don't want—"

"I grow tired," said Otuo, "of how often you talk about what *you* want." There was an edge to his voice that felt like a shiv against my throat. That was new.

NINETEEN

Otuo was gone by the time Liana and Cassie emerged. Cassie lugged her suitcase and Liana had produced another signal-blocking bag for Cassie's phone—or perhaps Cassie had already owned such a bag? That would have been in keeping with her personality. She gave Liana a hug before climbing into her car and laying a piece of paper down on the dashboard. A printout of the directions to the spa.

Normally I'd be concerned about sending her on her own to a place that was designed to be hard to find. Unbeknownst to her, though, Mouse was sitting in the back seat. She'd be able to watch over Cassie without agitating her OCD.

"What's the matter?" Liana asked me as she stepped up beside me.

Cassie was pulling her car out of the driveway, waving at Liana with a forced grin. She waved back.

"Seriously," Liana pressed, "you look like you've eaten a whole jar of dill pickles."

"I like dill pickles."

"Corban, answer the question."

"It's order stuff," I said. "You want to talk to your friends?"

"Huh?"

"Otuo says he's got a secure way for you to talk to your friends."

"Cool."

"So let's go."

"Yeah, sure, let's just drop the previous subject." She didn't move, only stood with her arms folded across her chest. I sensed that she was on the verge of laughing at me.

I looked up at the cloudless blue sky, then shut my eyes. "The order is in danger. I don't know details."

"Because of Darissa's attacks, still?"

"Those didn't help."

"Is Otuo, like, in charge of the order or something?"

"He's in the inner circle."

"What's that?" She quirked an eyebrow.

Something I shouldn't talk about with mortals, I thought.

"Corban…" She took me by the shoulders.

The responsible thing to do was shrug and pull away, but that wasn't going to happen. Her touch felt grounding. Her whole being radiated security. I didn't want her to let go. If she wanted to hug me, I was okay with that, too.

"The inner circle is a group of angels who know the secrets of our history," I said. "They know a fuller story of what we are and where we come from."

"Oh."

I shrugged. "They operate independent of our ruling council and occasionally overrule it. Otuo wants me to join them." I braced myself for an onslaught of questions.

"Oh. Okay." Liana let go of me.

That was it?

"You hungry?" she asked.

Was I? I could always eat food, it seemed like, these days. "I know you want to get to where you can talk to your friends." I started towards the car.

"The burger joint has a drive through."

She'd named the one place that I'd been thinking of. I could never recall the actual name of it; it wasn't part of a chain, but rather a local business that had bought an old chain-restaurant property and managed to make food that was even more processed and generic. Truly great stuff.

"That place still open?" I asked.

"Uh, is the world still spinning? Yeah, it's open. Where else would people go with their hangovers at four in the morning?" She swayed to one side, bumping into me on purpose. "Let's go. You drive?"

"People don't just go there with hangovers," I said as I got into the car.

"That's nice," said Liana. "Whatever else people go there to deal with, it's none of my business." Her upbeat mood from helping her aunt was intact, despite my sourness.

SO... ONCE I took a real look at the burger place's drive through, I had to admit that Liana had a point. The speaker we ordered from leaned at a crazy angle either from getting hit once by a truck, or a whole bunch of times by a whole lot of cars. The scrapes along the wall between the speaker and the window lent weight to the latter theory. Huge chunks of brown stucco had fallen away to reveal the cinderblock underneath. (Everything in Taos was stucco or adobe. Northern New Mexicans considered mud dwellings a status symbol—stucco was what they resorted to if they couldn't afford the real deal.)

Seriously, though, how drunk did one have to be to fail at navigating a drive through?

Liana all but climbed over me to grab the bag of food as the fast food worker held it out. I leaned back to avoid getting touched.

Well, to avoid getting touched skin to skin. Feeling her side press against mine and the softness of her breast against my arm was rather nice.

"Drive," she ordered me as she sat back down and dug through the bag.

It was a good twenty minutes or more to the Ski Valley, which was, as one would expect, high up in the mountains. It made sense that Otuo had set up whatever equipment he was using for a secure link to Turkey there, and I suspected that once we got to that little hamlet, we'd end up climbing higher or maybe taking the ski lift to the peak. That was the most obvious place to transmit a signal from.

Liana unwrapped my burger and handed it to me before munching away at hers. "You do have the most disgusting eating habits," she said with her mouth half full. "I'm amazed you didn't have a heart attack when you lost your powers."

"It doesn't work like that."

"I know. And it also turns out that I can eat as much junk food as I want without adverse effects. I just don't because it's disgusting."

"Yeah, you're a fun date." The words were out before I'd fully considered them, and this was the second time I'd made this mistake. Four years ago I'd teased Liana about being no fun as a blind date because she was so adept at thinking of terrible things strangers might do to her. It had been clear then, from the way she'd gone quiet and turned away, that she hadn't found it funny.

Now was no different. She turned to look out the window, stung.

Well, it was different. It was different because she'd confessed to liking me, so I should have known better than to say anything that sounded like mockery.

"I'm sorry," I said.

"You're fine."

"No, I'm not. You know how not fine I am nowadays."

Liana snorted. "You like these burgers. You were never fine."

The way she joked with me cut me two ways. It made it clear she really was getting over me, and that just plain hurt. It was like watching a mini-death, and knowing that a relationship couldn't ever be viable didn't make that death any easier to watch. It also highlighted, yet again, how compatible we were, and how easy it would have been to be her boyfriend if only I could touch her without risking the fate of the planet.

Even the way she sat in the passenger seat, with her shoes off and her feet tucked under her as she ate her burger, made my heart ache.

I drove the rest of the way through Taos itself, noting that the place hadn't changed much, or at all, really, since I'd been here last. It remained a small huddle of adobe buildings that fanned out into more spaced out stucco and adobe buildings, surrounded by really, really spread out adobe buildings on ranches. We drove away from the high density part of town and out into the desert before the road took us up into the mountains with their tall-pine-forest-covered slopes. The sun beat down with high-altitude intensity.

"But is it especially hard right now?" Liana asked, as if there hadn't been a ten minute gap in the conversation. "Holding it together?"

"Yeah."

"I'm sorry. Did dealing with my aunt make it worse?"

"Taos is making it worse," I said. "Lots of memories here."

"Oh… yeah… I forget that you were here so much longer than I was. I'm a self-centered mortal."

No, I thought, no you're not. You're the center of all my thoughts, too. I had lived here for decades and helped hundreds of people at the high school—probably thousands, but there was only one who stood out to me.

I finished my burger without really tasting it and drove on up the scenic, mountain road to the Ski Valley, which was almost deserted at this time of year. It wasn't a town I knew all that well, as there hadn't been many high schoolers who lived here. The place was basically a small collection of ski lodges and Alpine-themed hotels.

A single paved road went in a loop through the town, but, following directions Otuo had given me, we turned off it onto a gravel road that went into the trees. I'd say it took us to the edge of town, which I suppose it did, but the fire station was also on this gravel road. We drove past that and up a steep slope to a hotel which had a log-cabiny look to it, rather than the Alpine chalet theme. It was built on the slopes of the mountain and its buildings were on stilts to keep them level. Otuo was loitering by the big wooden sign proclaiming the place the "Snow Bear Inn."

So when I parked, he was right there to lead us around to the main building.

Liana stayed close to me, which I both liked and hated. I wanted to put my arm around her again, but settled for a hand on her shoulder.

Otuo led us onto a walkway that skirted the building and provided stunning views of the pine-clad slopes of the surrounding mountains. The air up here smelled fresher, with a slight hint of vanilla. The Ponderosa pines that grew all around had vanilla extract in their bark. It gave me flashbacks to seeing Liana at Princeton, her skin smelling softly of vanilla.

Liana kept her eyes focused on the room numbers of the doors we passed, though, and when we stopped in front of one, she bounced on the balls of her feet.

"Go on in," Otuo told her.

She knocked on the door and it burst open a second later, disgorging Amy and Gina in a flurry of waving hands and shrieks. They pounced on her, hugging her tight.

"Wait," I said.

"Yes, well," said Otuo, "as I said back at Cassie's house, we should talk."

Siobhan sauntered out after her charges and fixed me with an amused look. "So, now that we don't have to worry about eavesdroppers, do you mind telling me what the bloody hell is going on?"

"Why aren't they in Turkey?" I asked.

Otuo gave Siobhan a look that was pure poison. Something was very, very wrong.

TWENTY

Siobhan gave Otuo a cool look and turned to me.

"We've evaded Melanie," she said. "She fell for the second decoy flight to Turkey after she figured out the first decoy was a decoy. There have been goons patrolling around a fake safe-house near the Citadel for days, and no one followed us here."

"So, wait, what does that mean?" asked Liana. "I'm not going to Turkey?" She pulled back from the tangle of the group hug.

"No," said Siobhan.

"Definitely not," said Gina.

Otuo was clearly not happy with this. "Siobhan," he said, "has decided to defy the order. To defy the inner circle, even."

"The order is doomed," said Siobhan.

"That is preposterous," Otuo snapped.

"Agreed," I said.

"There are some things you need to know," said Siobhan.

"What kind of things?" I asked, glancing to make sure Amy and Gina were ignoring us as if we weren't present. To them, we weren't right now. "Things like us all being half-turned demons, like Liana?"

I hoped Siobhan would laugh or give me a strange look.

Instead, she shut her eyes and gave a terse nod. "How did you find out?"

Liana shot her a guilty look.

I kept my feet planted and folded my arms. "So it's true?"

"Corban…" Siobhan shook her head. "We really do need to talk. Somewhere private."

Otuo's expression grew even more severe. "This is insubordination."

"Yes, I'm aware of that," said Siobhan. "You don't need to be giving me lectures on the terminology. I've led armies. Corban, I'm putting my faith in you now."

"Then you're insane," I said. "I'm the last person you should be following right now."

"But—"

"I'm on the verge of falling."

"Fine, I still—"

"It's not *fine*."

"You nearly died. Is it surprising you're off-balance? I'm not surprised."

"I'm off-balance because I broke my covenants," I said. "I didn't kiss Liana just to save her life. I wanted her. I still want her." And with that I turned on my heel and marched off.

"Corban!" Otuo snapped.

Gina and Amy were oblivious to the drama. They continued to hug Liana, which also served to pin her down.

I marched to the end of the walkway, then broke into a run.

BECAUSE I'D STORMED off so fast, I hadn't had the chance to ask Siobhan why she'd brought the girls to Taos Ski Valley, a place that Melanie could discover easily and would likely scout out as she traced the footsteps of her dead sister. Then again, if all my records had been expunged from the order, perhaps she didn't know that. Perhaps she'd chosen it because it was close to Cassie's house but separate and apart at the same time.

I was being irresponsible, leaving Liana behind like this, but I was too angry to care. As usual, I was hungry, starving. Only the desertedness of this little hamlet kept me from salivating after some poor, innocent human going about their business.

When Liana went unstable, I could restore her with a touch. There was no such cure available to me.

As far as I knew, at least. If I really was fighting off demonic possession like Liana, then how was I doing it? What kinds of things held the demon at bay?

My steps slowed from a run to a jog and then to a walk.

Angels fell when we broke our covenants—or, that was the general belief. Not all angels were Christians, so not all thought of things in terms of covenants. Some instead committed to ideals, for example, or adopted humanitarian philosophies. Nevertheless, all members of the order had a concept of keeping the golden rule and the belief that serving humans was the highest calling that we were to follow above all others.

Serving humans meant feeding off them in a way that benefitted them, while fallen angels caused as much human pain as possible.

In a way, Liana did the same thing. She hadn't made formal covenants, but she did insist on doing what she felt was right at all times. She never fed on humans, but then again, her form of feeding never benefitted them in any way.

Was my restricted feeding part of how I fought off the demon? Was it also why I'd been needing sleep and food, lately? Was that me becoming more human? Like Liana?

I was confused. Two days ago I'd believed I was part of a different order of creation, a class of creatures crafted by God to serve humanity. Being chosen to ascend meant being chosen by God to live a higher existence. Vampires, on the other hand, were cursed by God, people who'd made a decision so unforgivable they forfeited their soul, caused God to withdraw His grace, and unleashed the powers of hell on Earth.

That had been my unshaken belief until I met Liana. Seeing her half-turned, her sense of morality intact, had caused me to evolve in my opinion. There hadn't been much time to decide what to do with her, but when I sensed her emotions were human and her heart was good, I knew that I needed to protect her as I would any human.

But I never thought I'd have to apply that judgment to myself. I'd ascended out of a pure desire to help humanity. Or had I? I'd also been sentenced to death, and this enabled me to live on.

The way I saw it, though, I *had* died and put off the chance to go to the afterlife in order to stay on Earth and help the rest of humanity make their own way to their maker. Was that selfish?

In my heart of hearts, I didn't think so.

Had Liana been at all selfless when she let Evan try to turn her? It was hard to say. She judged herself so harshly that the way she told the story was that she was silly and weak and thought she was in love. She'd also said that Evan told her he needed her help to defeat his sire, Darissa, and in the end, Liana had, indeed, killed her. Was the selfless desire to help her undeserving, demonically possessed boyfriend what had initially kept her soul in her body?

Or was it simply that God had forgiven a momentary lapse— requiring Liana to pay dearly by living a strict life, but accepting her repentance all the same? Meeting Liana had caused my world to tilt, and now I felt like I was on the deck of a rapidly sinking ship, having it list so far that any minute I'd lose traction and go plunging into the unfathomable depths.

I stopped walking and took a deep breath. I wasn't like Liana in a lot of ways, and yet right now, I felt like she was the one person who understood me.

Someone scuffed their feet to let me know they were approaching. I looked up, hoping to see Liana, but found it was Siobhan instead. She looked me over as she stepped up beside me. "Liana said I might find you here."

Huh? I looked around and realized I was in front of the strip mall with the urgent care center where Darissa had taken Liana to run some tests, only to have Liana kill her. It was where our friendship had come to its both untimely and overdue end. Liana knew me too well.

"Needless to say," said Siobhan, "we didn't know about the history of this place, or else we never would have brought the girls here."

"My records were expunged from the order."

"Yes they were. The order's gone off the rails."

"It may have been Darissa who did that. It suits her style."

"It was the order, Corban. The council did it to cover up this whole Liana debacle."

"Oh…"

"Like I said, they've gone off the rails. Which means you're all Liana's got, and you were horribly cruel to her just now."

"Yeah… I know."

"You two are going to have to talk. You can't tell a girl that you want her and then just run off."

"I'm sure she had some idea."

"I'm sure she didn't," Siobhan countered. "Look, I know you well enough not to think you're all that, but a mortal girl? Be fair."

I rolled my eyes while my old friend laughed. "I do have novelty value," I acknowledged. "But she's getting over me. Which is good."

Siobhan stepped into my line of sight, her arms folded across her chest. "Be honest. Do you want her in some unholy, lustful, debased way? Do you dream of hurting her for your own pleasure or anything like that?"

I shook my head and suppressed a shudder. "Never."

"Then I don't think she's what's got you off balance."

"Well, I do want her physically," I confessed. "So it's not entirely righteous."

At that my old friend flung up her hands and rolled her eyes. "You were in this bloody country too long. Honestly, Americans and their puritanical nonsense. It's not wrong to want someone physically."

"It is if it can never be."

"Is it? So if you were disabled and could never have a physical relationship with her because of your disability, that'd be evil? Unrighteous? You shouldn't want things you can't have even if the reason you can't have them isn't your fault at all?"

I opened my mouth, then shut it again. The first response that came to mind was that I wasn't disabled, but that was both not the point, and possibly not even true.

"Have you considered that maybe loving that girl is the one thing you're doing right, you clodpole?" Siobhan didn't call me names often.

I held up a hand to cut her off from hurling any more. "I have some practical questions," I said. "Is Liana immortal, like us? And if she is, is that why the order doesn't want to protect her? Because she's only as human as we are?"

Siobhan shook her head. "Well, I can't explain the order's actions, but the rest of it I can tell you, of course."

TWENTY-ONE

Siobhan and I standing in the parking lot painted a clear picture of how absurd the life of an angel was sometimes. The parking lot was gravel, and yet my friend wore stiletto heels, a tulip skirt, and a blouse unbuttoned to the third button. Most would find her sexy, and I suppose I did too. There was a difference between noticing someone was attractive and finding them attractive in a way that made me want to do something about it, though. She was no Liana, and the relentless urge to ogle women that had flared up during my time as a mortal had waned to the point that it was easy to ignore.

Siobhan was a good friend, helping me out in my darkest hour, though I was getting ever more frustrated by how long this "hour" of my life was. It had begun when I'd first been banished from seeing Liana, and I didn't see an end anytime soon.

"Liana is mortal," said Siobhan. "She may have the same blood tests as us, but she's got different cell cultures. In us, the symbionts are fully integrated and cause eternal regeneration.

Liana doesn't have that, so she will age and carry on like a regular human. Liana says Darissa did a cheek swab on her. I'm guessing that's what Darissa wanted to check for."

"She has the prettiness, though." I regretted the words the moment I spoke them. Her beauty wasn't what I cared about. It was artificial.

Siobhan didn't bat an eye. "Yeah, I'm not sure what's biology and what's magic, or if that's even a meaningful distinction."

"Pretty sure if there was one, I wouldn't understand it."

"You have the strangest form of wisdom," said Siobhan. "Believing you know so little is how you master so much."

I didn't understand what she meant, and didn't care to figure it out just now.

"Previous attempts to make half-turned vampires failed because we let the vampirism advance too far," said Siobhan.

"We've tried to make half-turned vamps?"

"Of course we have. You ready to hear some of the secrets of the inner circle?"

I put my hands in my pockets and let my shoulders drop. "It's not allowed. I'm not in the inner circle."

"Telling you is the right call. My mentor would agree."

"Who's your mentor?"

"You."

I rolled my eyes. "I reserve judgment there, but fine, tell me."

"When our kind first came to Earth, we nearly destroyed humanity. It was only fallen angels back then, none half-turned, and we wrought havoc. Beings like that against humanity still in the stone age? They didn't stand a chance, except that it was a human who figured out how to defeat fallen angels. He figured out how to stay half-turned by choosing not to do what the demon wanted him to do. Morality was a concept humans understood, but it was still rather undeveloped at the time."

"Was he our founder?"

"Yes."

"Was it Otuo?"

"Yeah. But he's really cagey about anyone knowing that. Some of the inner circle believe our founder was Adam, and he does not want to be called that. He also doesn't ever want to talk about what happened to his wife, so we have no idea if she was anything like Eve. But symbolically, she might have been. Eve's the one recorded making the first ever moral choice in the Bible, and maybe she went and got turned on purpose so that she could find a strategy to cope with the demon invasion. You know me, though, I'm not a literalist about any of that stuff."

"How much of what you know is contrary to our faith?" I asked.

"None. I know things that complicate my beliefs—"

"Us being demons is contrary to our faith."

She shook her head. "No it's not. We already knew Lucifer was a fallen angel. Us being capable of destroying humankind and damning them to eternal suffering is not a new concept. It was the invasion of the fallen angels that forced humanity to embrace concepts of morality and cultivate them, to take the warfare up a conceptual level, to turn to higher powers however they could, to search for universal rules that would enable them to prevail against an enemy that had every physical advantage.

Those are the same principles that set humans apart from all other creatures, their ability to think in abstraction. That's what allows humans to form societies and nations and systems of justice. Otuo and his order of half-turned demons lived openly among humans for millennia, helping them along, until a few thousand years ago when we decided to all go undercover. We helped humanity rise above being mere beasts to the beings they are today, and nowadays they're advancing by leaps and bounds because of the abstract concepts that are now second nature to them."

"But what was the religion back in Otuo's time?"

"I don't know." She shrugged. "Perhaps no one does, not after all the times we've lost our scholars. Otuo may have been around back then, but you know how memories work when you're ancient. They fade. As for where religion came from and when humans adopted it…" She shrugged. "Christ preached a lot of practices that beat demonkind back to the point where demonic possession is now a fringe belief. You can think he was just a clever man, or you can think that he had access to higher, eternal truths that have always been with humanity. It's the same choice everyone has to make about him."

I let that sink in. "But he's not around, that anyone knows of? He didn't ascend to be like us?"

"No," said Siobhan. "What happened in his ascension is a mystery. Your guess is as good as mine."

Well, I'd long believed that to be true, so I didn't feel let down there. The rapidly tilting world tilted a little less rapidly now.

"Anyway, yes," she said, "we tried to conquer vampires by trying to create half-turned ones."

"The tamer of demons shall set them free?"

"Ye-es, takes on an interesting meaning, doesn't it? Otuo taught us how to tame our demons, and by extension developed the philosophies that allow humans to tame their demons, literal and figurative. He set us all free."

"Or could it be Liana?"

Siobhan inclined her head. "Interesting… It could be both. You know how prophecies work. There are often multiple fulfillments, some major, some minor. Like all the martyrs that came before and have been since Christ. But if it applies to Liana too, that means she's still got to set her kind free somehow."

"Maybe that's why she didn't die after killing Darissa. Her work wasn't done yet."

"I don't know. Failure is always an option. Maybe she didn't die because she's as bloody stubborn as you are. You aren't about to die either, not the Corban I know."

"You don't know what it's like for me right now."

"This is true, but I do know you. I've known you for how long now? Six hundred years? Since you found me naked as a jaybird in an Irish winter fighting four vampires I'd baited out of their lair?"

I chuckled. "You were avenging the death of your husband."

"Corban, nobody else, angel or human, would have come to my rescue. Only you saw that situation and decided there was more to the story."

"Anyone would have known there was more to the story."

"Aside from me being a raving lunatic." Her eyes twinkled with amusement.

"There are perfectly good, sound reasons for a person to become a raving lunatic," I said, "and your raving laid all those reasons out quite well."

"Only you would have listened, and I suspect you're one of only a few who really, truly understands." She smiled as if she'd just scored a point.

I didn't follow.

"I was driven to madness by love for my husband. I was trying to avenge his death. Being willing to do anything for love, even take on crazy, losing fights, that was what made me able to ascend. Because that's our job, to do anything for love. You and I believe it's the love of God's children. I can't wait to see my husband in the hereafter, and yet I can wait because while I wait, I'm fighting good fights and learning ever more about love, about how deep and strong a force it is. You saw that potential in me. Not everyone would. Did you know I was the youngest person to ever join the inner circle?"

I shook my head. "I didn't."

"Do you know that nearly everyone in the inner circle was helped to ascend by you?"

"I'm not supposed to know who's in the inner circle."

"Well, you've turned enough people, that doesn't narrow it down by much. The thing is, you've got a good eye. You spot not just the righteous, but the valiant, and I don't think it was coincidence that you helped all of us, and I don't think it was coincidence that you were the one to find Liana."

"Then why is every day such a struggle?"

"Because bad things happen to good people? It's a fallen world? You know the answers. The only reason you're asking the question is because you're so careful not to do the wrong thing. I get that's part of your process, but for what it's worth, I don't think you're doing anything wrong. Someone who miraculously survives cancer may still have to deal with the damage the disease and treatment did to their body. Someone who survives kissing a vampire may be in a similar situation." She leaned in as she said this, as if to press the point home. "And a lot of us are struggling these days. Nobody fully knows why."

"I dunno."

"It's very interesting that you survived kissing a vampire, and that both of you became more human afterwards."

I folded my arms. Her logic was tempting, so my instinct was to reject it.

"You're in uncharted territory," she said. "You shouldn't accept the conclusions other people jump to, not at a time like this."

Siobhan had always been a risk-taker, though. It made her deadly on the battlefield, but a bit of a loose cannon in every other situation. I wasn't like her, and I didn't particularly want to be.

The sound of a car approaching gave me an excuse to look away, and I was startled to see a familiar Suburban with its uncannily young, female driver.

"You!" Siobhan shouted when the girl pulled up and rolled down her window. "You're following us?"

"Wait, you too?" I asked. "I thought she was following us."

The girl leaned an arm out the window and looked the two of us over. "I'm trying to find that ferrum worker I talked to in the airport," she said.

"Why?" Siobhan demanded, her chest puffing out as she shifted into protector mode.

"Because I have more ferrum," the girl replied.

TWENTY-TWO

"**F**errum is from the demon realm!" Otuo ranted when we got back to the hotel room. Gina and Amy were lounging on the bed and Liana was nowhere to be seen. Siobhan explained that they'd set up ferrum amulets to shield a block of three rooms, and Liana was alone in hers. I knew I needed to go find her, but I couldn't exactly leave in the middle of this conversation, and if I was being honest with myself, I wasn't ready to face her just yet.

The room was done up in Earth tones with art featuring wildlife and mountain vistas—a very effective, idealized version of a mountain cabin. It was strange, therefore, how out of place a coyote-shifter looked in here. She stood in one corner as if we'd backed her there, but kept her chin up.

Siobhan and I shut the door behind us. Otuo, who had been sitting at a table in the corner, was now on his feet, jaw clenched and hands balled into fists.

Because there was a non-angel in this conversation, Gina and Amy could overhear us, and the looks on their faces were pure bafflement.

"Sorry," I said to them. "You don't have to stay. This conversation is going to get weird."

"You two must leave now," said Otuo.

They exchanged a look.

"So it's true," said Amy. "You guys aren't human."

"What gave it away?" I asked.

"Corban!" Otuo snapped.

"You're too good looking," said Gina. "And you have way too much power and money and… whatever. We figured the order had to be something more than just an old human institution."

"But you aren't vampires?" Amy asked.

"They're the same kind of demon," said the coyote-girl, "but a different form of possession. These guys are what you would call angels."

Hearing that from someone outside of the order was like a hard slap upside the head. I couldn't help but gape at her. How long had her kind known this about us? I didn't even bother to wonder if it was correct. Too much evidence was stacking up in its favor.

Gina and Amy exchanged a look of confusion, but asked nothing more. I suppose Otuo was making it clear that he wanted them to shut up.

Now, he glowered at the coyote.

I turned back to her. "There's a demon realm?" I asked. I felt like I was betraying Liana, having this conversation without her. "Is it like the other worlds that other supernaturals come from?"

"You two, out," said Otuo, pointing at the door.

Gina and Amy scampered off, letting the door swing shut behind them.

"Yes," said Siobhan. "The demon realm is like the other worlds supernaturals come from."

"No it's not," said the girl.

Otuo and Siobhan blinked at her in surprise.

The door swung open again and Amy, Gina, and Liana came marching in.

"Get out," said Otuo.

"Just… they need to know this stuff," I said.

Liana kept her jaw set and her gaze turned decisively away from me.

I turned my gaze away as well, hoping this came off as polite. She probably knew me well enough to know it was cowardice, though.

The coyote-girl brightened at once. "Hi!" she said.

"Hi," said Liana. "Nice to see you again."

"Thanks for the cash."

"Yeah, of course." Liana shrugged.

"Vampires don't do that, you know? When you offered it to me, I was, like, this girl is so not a vampire."

"I'll take that as a compliment." Liana climbed onto the bed with her friends, the three of them lined up side by side, lounging against the pillows. It was another "three cultures of New Mexico" publicity shot.

"Wait," said Amy. "Did I hear you guys talking about other worlds?"

"There are other worlds people live in," I told her. "And that is literally all I know. I've never been to one."

"I mean, like, the demon realm is another world," the coyote-shifter said. "It's another world that you reach by portal, but it's, like, off limits. Nobody's allowed to portal there."

"Portal?" Gina asked.

"Yeah," said the girl. "That's, like, how you get to other worlds besides this one. Through portals."

Gina bit her lip, considering that.

"So where did you get the ferrum?" Otuo demanded.

"Like, we kept a small stockpile of it."

"Who is *we?*" Siobhan demanded, glaring around at us.

"Okay, let's back up," I said. "How do you guys know this girl?" I pointed to the coyote-shifter.

"She came up to me in the airport and admired my rings," said Gina. "Asked what they were made out of, and I said it was a rare form of steel."

"And I asked if you wanted more of that metal," said the shifter-girl.

"And I said sure," said Gina, "because I thought you were a weirdo and I was joking." Gina wasn't the most patient person in the world as it was, and her tone indicated that she was on the brink of snapping.

I couldn't blame her. This was testing the bounds of how much weirdness I could digest.

Fortunately, the shifter-girl seemed pretty unflappable. All she did was shrug with one shoulder and say, "Well, I wasn't joking."

"So you found Gina at the airport," I said, "and got a request for more ferrum. Why did you start following us?"

"Well, like... I can't track someone like her." She nodded towards Gina. "And angels are too common. That also makes them hard to track. But I can track that vampire girl, of course." She nodded at Liana.

"Of course?" asked Otuo.

"Uh, yeah, obviously. You're demon carriers." She looked at us as if no further explanation was necessary.

I mentally put a pin in that point and moved on. "So you found us heading across the country and followed us?"

"Yeah. And you, like, led me back to the ferrum workers."

"How did you know we had anything to do with each other?" I asked.

The girl raised an eyebrow. "Um... who else is gonna need ferrum? Obviously the only people who need ferrum and ferrum workers are, like, people about to go to war with some powerful vampires."

"But how did you know to find me in the first place?" Gina asked. "Why didn't you just go bother Liana?"

"Because right then, there was an angel in town I could follow. After all those vampires got killed, I assumed she had something to do with it. When I saw there was a ferrum worker, then I knew it was something bigger than the usual skirmish."

"And then did you get permission from your kind to deliver us more ferrum?" Otuo asked.

"Yeah, we don't really do, like, permission or coordination or stuff like that. That's totally not how we are."

Siobhan folded her arms. "So there's a chance we could have more of your kind show up at any minute, demanding to know what happened to your ferrum stockpile?"

"Uh, no." The girl almost laughed, but didn't. "Most of my kind are going to stay the hell away from all of you guys, obviously."

Everyone began to talk then, but I held up a hand. "I think it's safe to say that things that are obvious to you may be quite obscure to us. Our peoples haven't worked together in centuries."

"Obviously."

Gina snickered.

I made myself rein in my temper. At least she had me so intrigued that I wasn't distracted by the fact that I was in a room with three humans whom I could torture and feed upon. Siobhan's close proximity might have had something to do with that too. I wouldn't get very far if I stepped out of line. She'd fell me on the spot.

"Why is that obvious?" I asked.

"Okay, can I just ask what she *is*?" Amy interjected.

"A coyote." The girl gave her a cool look.

"Oh," said Amy. "So you ferry people back and forth between… other worlds?"

"No," I began.

"Yeah," said the girl.

Otuo and Siobhan both looked thunderstruck (and I likely did as well, but I tried to keep my cool). "Wait," I said, "what? I… thought you were a shifter."

"Like… I can turn into the animal too, yeah, but the name obviously is from my ability to take people between worlds."

This was the last straw. "That is not obvious!" I shouted. "None of this is obvious."

"Well, like, she thought it was." The girl nodded towards Amy.

"It's just that you talked about the demon realm being off limits," said Amy, "and that implied it was a place you could get to."

"Fine," I said, turning to the girl again. "Is there something our kind did to your kind back in the day that means you never talk to us about this stuff?"

"You guys are a total abomination."

"Obviously," Gina quipped, "but spell it out for us, okay?"

The girl panned the room with her gaze.

"You're safe here," I said. "Say what you need to say."

TWENTY-THREE

"So, like, okay... you guys know nothing about portalling?" the coyote-girl asked, now seated in the chair Siobhan had pulled out for her. Her posture was more relaxed and there was a hint of amusement in her eyes.

It took a very strange person to be amused by this.

We all shook our heads. It wasn't true that I knew *nothing* about portalling, but for the purposes of this conversation, it was best to start from zero and not skip over anything this girl thought was "obvious."

"Okay, so... like, there are other worlds connected to this one. The way you get to them is through portals. Sometimes people have the power to portal on their own."

"How?" Gina asked. "Is it something they inherit?"

The girl shrugged. "Um, like... there are a lot of rules. Sometimes it's to fulfill a prophecy or something, but you know, it can be all kinds of reasons."

Okay… so we were apparently going to blow right past a discussion of prophecies that linked people to other worlds. This was sure to be a wild ride.

The coyote-girl paused and looked at us each in turn. "So… my people are the only ones who can cross into any world, and who can take people with us. That's why we keep to ourselves. Too many people want to control us."

"I get that," said Amy. "You can trust us."

The girl shrugged. She had decided to trust us when she approached Gina. "Like, okay, so that's how it's supposed to work when people cross over from other realms. The problem with the demon realm is that it, like, totally doesn't work like that. Demons started invading Earth, like, billions of years ago. Okay, not billions, but, like, a really long time ago."

"Your people remember the Angel Wars too, then?" Otuo asked, giving the rest of the room an uneasy look. "You keep records?"

"Yeah…" said the coyote, "so we were created by magic to try to stop the demon invasion."

Otuo shifted his weight; I got the impression this was not new information to him.

"The Angel Wars," coyote-girl continued, "had been going on forever, and so some magic users who knew about portals created a spell that would allow people to portal anywhere they wanted. Obviously, that spell doesn't take very often. My kind is pretty rare."

"Stop," said Gina. "What the heck does that mean?"

"It's, like, a standing spell," said the girl.

"Like the spells on homes that keep vampires out?" Liana asked.

"Yeah, exactly."

When her two friends both leaned forward to stare at her, Liana explained, "The reason vampires can't enter a home uninvited is because of spells. There are a few different spells and several ways to activate them, but as I understand it, they were cast a long time ago and just... persist."

"They persist as long as the Oaths are kept," said the coyote. "Which is, like, a Sidhe thing."

"Obviously," said Amy, dryly.

"Let me see if I understand," I cut in. "The spell that creates your kind is a standing spell that takes effect... when you're born?"

"Um, I guess so. I mean, we are born as we are, but we don't inherit our abilities. Like, our parents won't have them."

Well, that explained why coyote-shifters were such loners.

"Which world is your kind from?" Liana asked.

"Like... all of them? Except the demon realm. So, like, the creators of the spell cast the spell thingy and then it took a few hundred years before they found the first member of my kind. I dunno if that's the first time the spell took or what, but once my kind started to show up, they collected, like, a small band of us and asked us to see if we could go into the demon realm and stop these spirits coming over."

"Okay, pause," said Liana. "That's how vampirism happens? Demons are spirits that cross over from the demon realm?"

The girl nodded. "Vampirism and angel… ism? However you say it. Which is totally, like, not how it's supposed to work. Spirits without bodies aren't supposed to leave their own realms, you know?"

I did not know that, but decided to let it slide.

"So, like, my kind took an expedition into the demon realm and we learned some stuff. Like, we learned that the people in that realm were all messed up. We also had some regular people with us, and when we brought them back, one of 'em was wearing a metal bracelet from the demon realm, and he got in a fight with an angel and smacked 'em with it. It left a burn. That's how we figured out that metal from the demon realm hurt demon possessed people in this realm, and only those people who'd been to the demon realm and back and their descendants could work the metal."

"That's what we are?" Amy asked, gesturing to herself and Gina. "Descendants of the people who portalled over and back?"

"Yeah."

"What happened to them?" Gina asked.

"The people who portalled over and back? They lived in Iberia, had a civilization there that was, like, annihilated and some of their descendants survived and are still around."

Obviously, I added in my mind. Well, that explained why so many New Mexicans were ferrum workers. The conquistadors had come from the Iberian Peninsula, after all.

"Anyway," said the coyote-girl, "we did some more expeditions to get more metal so that people could make, like, weapons and armor and stuff, but we had to stop when we figured out that portalling somehow was letting even more demons out of the realm, and we were thinning the barrier between worlds and one of the angels did… something while the portal was open."

Otuo shifted his weight again, his eyes narrowing, his temper building.

"She got some magic users to cast a spell to try to send her demon back to the demon realm, but all it did was change the way she was possessed. That's how you guys got vampires. There were only angels before, and cuz vampirism spreads so fast… we decided it was best to close the portal at that point. I mean, someone did. We're not sure who exactly did it. It didn't work; the demons still invade."

I couldn't help but look at Liana, and caught her gaze just as she flicked it away. "So, wait," she said. "What's the demon realm like? You said it was all messed up. Are there actual demons over there with horns and tails, or what?"

"No, they're just weird people."

"Weird how?" Gina asked.

"Like… they've got glowing skin and black eyes and their world has no sun." She shrugged. "It's the starlight kingdom."

At that, every angel and vampire in the room went rigid with shock. Silence took hold, so profound that it rang.

Only Gina and Amy looked confused. "Sounds like the title of a Broadway musical," said Gina.

"The moon has risen over the starlight kingdom," said Liana.

"Yeah, like, the demons who come over have started saying that. It's weird." The coyote-girl shrugged. "So, anyway, all that's why the demon realm is off limits, and nobody remembers where the portal to it is anyway."

"It's… in Petra," said Amy.

My gaze darted to her.

Otuo's hands balled into fists.

"Where?" the girl asked.

"Um… I need to do a little more research." She pulled out what looked like a cell phone, but before I could get uptight, she said, "This thing doesn't send any signals anywhere. It's just loaded with stuff from your archives. Siobhan was able to get it for me instead of me getting to go to Turkey. I had some ideas when I did my senior thesis that I want to research a little more."

"What was your thesis in, again?" I asked.

"Cave dwellers. The Nabateans were weird because they were accomplished stoneworkers who embellished the outsides of caves, but not the insides."

"Because you think the cave mouths were portals?" asked Liana. "So the interiors didn't matter?"

"Yeah… I mean I don't know for sure, okay? But lemme study up."

Everyone exchanged looks of hope.

"Look, I don't mean to be rude," said the coyote-girl, "but I'm, like, starving. You guys got anything to eat?"

"Right," said Siobhan, remembering herself. "I'll go out and get you guys lunch. Let me find out what there is."

Otuo shook his head. "No, wait. No one leaves this room."

We all paused.

"You know this conversation has broken key covenants. Covenants make us what we are. I know you won't like doing this, but we need to kill the mortals who've been privy to our secrets. It's for the greater good."

The coyote-girl leapt to her feet and backed away. In a flash, she was gone.

The rest of the girls stared at Otuo in horror.

My old mentor seemed calm enough, but there was a telltale darkening in his eyes. It was something I hadn't seen for hundreds of years, but seeing it now sent a chill down my spine.

"We aren't killing the girls," I said.

"There are mysteries for a reason," Otuo argued. "We don't just go handing them out to children."

"Hey," I said, "we've had human allies all down through history. Right now we can use all the help we can get."

"Corban, it isn't your decision to make." Otuo turned his gaze on me. The whites of his eyes were definitely darkening. "It's not your place. *I* founded the order, and yet among you and your groupies, I get no respect."

"Whoa," said Liana, "So you really did found the order? When? How?"

"Uh…" I said. "I don't think he's in a mood to answer that kind of question. You'd better take your friends and go."

"I know what it's like to care for someone you can't be with," said Otuo. "I know that better than anyone."

Liana's ears pricked up, her gaze calculating.

"Go!" I shouted at her.

Otuo started towards me.

The girls all made a run for it.

TWENTY-FOUR

Liana, Amy, and Gina all made it out the door and ran a short ways, before there came the sound of another door slamming.

When I turned back around, Otuo was watching me with anger still clouding his features. I held up a hand, making it clear that if he went after them, he'd have me to contend with. I wasn't sure that this was much of a deterrent for him. Compared to him, I was an infant. He was the oldest immortal on the planet.

Siobhan, I noticed, was on her guard also. She hid it well—she always had. Anyone who fought her either learned fast that she could let loose a flurry of attacks without warning, or didn't live long. Rather than tense up, she relaxed, and rather than survey the room, she let her eyes unfocus while she gathered information from her peripheral vision.

Right now, I was doing the same thing.

"Calm down," I ordered him. "You're scaring people."

"You are in no position to judge me," he replied. The heat was gone from his voice, replaced instead by cold anger.

"I'm not judging—"

"You have just broken how many covenants?" he demanded. "And you chide me for being angry? What I feel is *righteous* indignation, old friend. There are times when we must kill people. You have to consider the absolute law!"

"Just… let's make sure that's true in this case," I pleaded. "Let's talk reasonably."

"I will not listen to you rationalize and justify all of the poor decisions you've made. Your betrayal puts the entire order at risk. And you—" he rounded on Siobhan "—you should never have been admitted to the inner circle. I told them that you were too young, too impetuous, but no. Angels turned by Corban are ever so popular. Your fire, your independence, all of you duped the rest of the circle into believing you were of a higher calling, able to discern truth even when most would be deceived. Your arrogance has torn the inner circle apart."

"I'm not wrong," she replied. "And Corban would have been more likely to join the inner circle if you didn't run it like a little cabal, answerable to no one but you."

"I am the founder of the order!" he repeated.

"Which is one of those secrets you're not supposed to let people like me know," I said. "For good reason. If more people knew that, they'd follow you no matter the mistakes you made. Or are making *right now*." That, I knew as soon as I'd said it, was a mistake. It wasn't my place to question someone like Otuo. I'd stayed out of the inner circle for precisely this reason; so that my judgments wouldn't have consequences much beyond myself.

"Corban," said Siobhan. "Ease up there, my friend."

If *she* was reining me in, then I knew I'd taken things way too far.

"Sorry," I said. "I am grateful to you for everything you've done for our kind."

Otuo turned away from me to face Siobhan. "You're bending the rules to justify your own wants. You don't want Corban to be unstable, so you tell yourself that his battles are acceptable, are righteous. He lusts after a demon, and you tell our secrets to mortals and break our ancient vow to the ferrum bloodline!"

"Liana needs protection," Siobhan replied. "The situation called for some extreme measures."

While I respected Siobhan's fire, I wished she'd be a little less like herself right now. She was ever the loose cannon, and this situation was sorely lacking anyone with a level head. I couldn't be that person right now...

Otuo stepped forward. "We cannot afford to break rules and bend our principles for one person, even if she does have a human soul."

"We cannot afford," Siobhan said, "to let our rules and usual practices justify cutting corners on the real work. The real work we do is saving souls, on an individual and case by case basis if necessary. You—"

The rest of her words were drowned out by a wordless roar from Otuo. "Justifications and rationalizations!" he bellowed. "How am I the only one who sees this? How have you—" he jabbed a finger at me "—managed to insinuate your way so deep into our ranks, causing a rot that will tear us apart?" His eyes darkened still more.

I hadn't ever been in the presence of an angel while they fell, but I'd been well briefed by those who had. It was time to run. Odds were Otuo would hold it together. He'd lived long enough that this seemed like too minor of a misunderstanding to push him over the edge. All the same, I was taking no chances. Not when Liana's safety relied on it.

Siobhan, sensing my decision, dropped into fighting stance, which made me pause.

"Go!" she shouted as she launched herself between me and Otuo.

I did not want to leave her there, but there were three mortal girls nearby who wouldn't last a second against a fallen angel. So I ran. I bolted out onto the walkway and opened the next door over. This room was empty. In the next one down, I found the three girls huddled together on the floor, next to the bed. "Come on," I told them.

Liana and Amy jumped to their feet, but Gina froze.

I couldn't blame her.

"Come on!" Liana said, dragging on her arm. "Move now!"

With a series of blinks, Gina sprang into motion, stumbling to her feet and following Amy out the door. I gestured for the three of them to run down the walkway, away from Otuo's room. This meant also running away from the entrance to the hotel and the road to town, but there was nothing to be done about that. Their feet made loud stomping sounds and the walkway trembled as they ran. I supposed it didn't matter if Otuo overheard our flight. He'd have known what I intended to do the moment I took off. It was then that I noticed Gina and Amy had their minds masked. Liana's work, most likely. Clever girl.

I sprinted after the three of them, keeping one eye on them and using the other to survey the area. There was a pretty long drop if we went over the railing, and it looked like that would be our only option once we ran out of walkway. There was no way we could stay in the hotel structure; that was sure to come down if Otuo couldn't hold it together.

If we went over the railing, that meant dropping down onto a steep slope and then rolling down into the parking lot. If we kept running, we'd soon run out of parking lot. "Guys!" I shouted. "Jump!"

The three of them skidded to a stop and peered down over the railing.

"Seriously?" Liana asked.

I nodded. "Now. Go. If you hurt yourselves, I'll heal you. Go!"

"Go guys." Liana hauled on Amy's shoulder, just as the wind picked up. Given where we were, it should have been a cool breeze, but it wasn't. It was scorching hot.

That pushed the girls into action. Gina went first, limbs flailing as she fell. She hit the hillside with a thud, but managed to roll. Amy jumped after her and landed farther up on the hill and also managed to roll.

Liana watched to make sure they were safe before vaulting down herself.

I leapt over the railing and for a small eternity, I fell, the hot air scorching my back as I descended down to the cool, natural air below. With a practiced bend of the knees, I landed in a squat in the parking lot and was able to be up and moving a split second later.

The three girls hadn't stopped to pick pine needles out of their hair or even brush themselves off. They were running towards the road. I ran after them. "Off the road!" I shouted. "Get into the trees!"

They all glanced back at me, their faces pale, but when I pointed down into the trees, they did what I asked. With some stumbles and oofs, they piled off the road.

If only the citizens of Rome had been this trusting. "Keep running," I ordered. "Fast as you can." I gestured that we keep on a trajectory that would take us neither downhill nor up. Down was where magma might flow. Up was where the hot gasses would scorch. The middle ground might just be survivable, and it was easier to run on, but not by much. Tree roots and rocks jutted up from the deep layer of pine needles, ready to trip anyone who wasn't careful.

A flash between the trees caught my eye and a coyote came crashing through the underbrush, making far more noise than a wild animal ever did. "Follow!" I ordered the girls.

They bent their steps to do so and the animal led us in a winding path, dashing through the trees. Someone was going to turn an ankle or crash into a tree trunk at any second, it was inevitable. And yet the girls ran.

When a deep rumble sounded behind us, they kept running.

When the coyote darted into a low cave, they dove in after it.

I hoped that we were following the right creature and not diving into the den of an actual, mother coyote. The mouth of the cave was narrow, and the cave itself not much wider. I squeezed into the pitch blackness, the cool air a shock against my skin, and used my body to cover the opening.

The ground began to shake, then I felt a blast of heat against my back. If I were human, I'd have blisters or worse. As it was, I felt uncomfortably hot and my shirt was set alight.

I did my best to pull it off—which was hard in the tiny cave that was full of elbows and knees—and stuff it out of the cave. The stink of brimstone saturated the air.

And then, it was over. The air cooled, the breeze blew, and I could turn my attention to the panting, terrified girls cowering in the darkness. "Everyone okay?" I asked.

"What happened?" Liana's voice.

"I think Otuo fell," I said.

"Then," came the coyote-girl's voice, "we need to get to my truck. It's full of ferrum weapons and is parked in the hotel parking lot."

"And Otuo knows that," I realized.

"We need to move now!" Her voice was shrill with urgency. "Please!"

TWENTY-FIVE

I backed myself out of the cave and peered through the trees towards the town, which was engulfed in smoke. As I stood there, the smoke cloud expanded, enveloping us, turning the serene forest into a netherworld that reeked of char and destruction. The air across the skin of my chest and back felt strange, like I was naked. It'd been a long time since I'd gone shirtless outside, and my days as a Roman, walking around fully nude at times, were deep in my past. My dagger sheath was the only clothing on my upper body and that felt strange.

Birds took flight, swarming out of the trees and flitting on up towards clearer air. Animals on the ground took off, some running, some bounding, each little more than a blur as they raced for their lives.

I took a deep breath of the choking haze and began to cough. I could barely see a few yards from where I stood; the town was now obscured.

Amy, then Gina, then Liana came worming out of the cave and came to stand with me, their shirts pulled up over their noses and mouths. That was smart of them.

The coyote-girl was the last out, and she squinted towards the town. "We need to go now," she repeated, her voice hoarse.

There was no way I was taking four mortals back to that devastation.

Liana, though, piped up. "I have a mylar blanket in my money belt. Amy, Gina, and I can stay in the cave and put that over us."

Amy nodded. "Yeah. You guys go." The arm that she used to wave me off with was scraped raw and seeping blood.

As I reached out to heal her, though, she shooed me away. "Later. We'll worry about that stuff later. Nobody's got life threatening injuries?"

"Nope," rasped Gina.

Liana shook her head.

Her two friends were already climbing back into the cave.

I did not like this at all. I wasn't sure what might happen next, but it seemed like those three ought to be getting as far away as possible. If they struck out on their own, though, they'd be exposed and unprotected.

The coyote-girl was in no position to plan strategy, either. She was on the verge of bolting towards the town, consequences be damned. Supernatural as she was, she was still human, in possession of a human soul for my purposes, and she was right that if Otuo got his hands on a stash of ferrum weapons, he could use them against us.

"Okay," I said. "You lead, I follow." A glance over my shoulder assured me that the Liana and her friends were inside the cave, as safe as possible for the moment.

That glance was all the time it took for the girl to shift into coyote form, and then she was off and running.

I pelted after her, wheezing in the smokey air, still unnerved at having so much skin exposed. A bolt of lighting lit up the forest around us so starkly that the image of trees with their long trunks and spindly branches was burned into my retinas. The sky ripped with the sound of thunder, which shook the ground so hard that I nearly lost my footing. I couldn't afford to do that. The coyote was disappearing fast into the smokey haze.

With my arms and legs pumping and my chin down, I put on a fresh burst of speed and reached the steep incline that I suspected led up to the road. My suspicion was confirmed a moment later when I burst out of the trees and onto the graded gravel.

The coyote was waiting for me, ears back and tail down.

Even though I was coughing up a storm, I waved for her to keep going and she set out at a trot as another bolt of lighting lit up the world around us, making the coyote's fur look a blinding white. The thunder made my ears hurt badly enough that I wondered if they would bleed. I couldn't hear anything for the ringing that followed. All I could do was focus on the coyote and follow her.

The trees on either side of the road opened up and I was staring at the sign for the Snow Bear Inn. The building was a smoking, burning skeleton with beams sticking up like charred ribs, and yet the Suburban and my rental car were still there in the parking lot. They were scorched and the paint peeling and blistered, but they weren't melted to slag.

Coyote-girl darted behind the Suburban and a moment later I saw her human form climb into the driver's seat.

I grabbed my keys out of my pocket and went for the rental car. If it had survived to this point and was still drivable, then it might still be useful to us. At the very least, it contained my and Liana's luggage. As I climbed into the seat, the upholstery against my back reminded me yet again that I was shirtless. The engine started without any problems, but when I threw it in reverse, it was obvious that at least three of the tires were flat.

Not a pressing issue.

The Suburban was also in reverse and I waited for its driver to put it in drive before I followed it back down the road that would take us out of town.

Bolts of lighting punched the ground around us as we made our escape, and my ears were so battered with noise that I felt more than heard the thunder. The car protested at me flooding the engine with gas and rocked and shimmied on its shocks, threatening to careen out of control as I gripped the steering wheel and focused on the dark splotch with twin red lights ahead of me—all I could see of the Suburban.

Another bolt of lighting struck to our right, illuminating a dark figure with wings that crackled with electricity, holding it aloft.

I averted my gaze. *Focus on driving*, I told myself.

The thunder sent a shockwave through the ground that tossed the car into the air. I sucked in my breath and grit my teeth as it came smashing down again, breaking the windows on the passenger side. Up ahead was the sign welcoming people to Taos Ski Valley, and I gunned towards it.

Just as I hit the curve in the road that took me out of the town and on down the mountain, I caught sight of the Suburban again. It was foundering, listing off to one side as two of its tires were now shredded rubber. Its brake lights lit up as the girl guided it to the side of the road.

I pulled up behind her and vaulted out of the driver's seat as the girl climbed, first into the back seat of her vehicle, and then back into the cargo area.

Before going to the Suburban, I went to open the trunk of my car. Yes, this was vanity, but it felt too weird to be bare-chested. I grabbed a shirt out of my suitcase and pulled it on while I shut the trunk. Boy did it feel good to have fabric against my skin again.

But I needed to keep moving. I pelted over to the Suburban and pried the back doors open, heedless of how hot the metal was and was able to just get my hands up in time to catch a duffel bag the coyote-girl tossed in my direction

It was full of metal, and knocked me back a few steps. If I'd been human, it would have knocked me out and left a lot of bruises to boot.

She came clambering out with another duffel back slung over her back. "There's one more!" she shouted, pointing.

I dove towards the third bag—dark blue rapidly turning gray as ash from the air rained down on us—hauled it out, tossed it over my shoulder, and then turned to follow the girl as she staggered back into the trees.

Once we were down off the road, she slowed her pace but kept going. I stepped up beside her. "This all of it?" I asked.

"Yeah. Thanks. Is he going to come for us, do you think?"

"I don't know, but assuming Siobhan survived, no. He'll have his hands full, fighting her." What Siobhan lacked in strength, she more than made up for in stealth and agility. Fighting her was like fighting four people at once; she came from every direction, blizzard fast. I'd accused her more than once of having vampire speed. That wasn't at all funny to me now.

"Okay…" The girl paused for another fit of coughing, before saying, "That angel woman is alive and she didn't fall. I can take the two mortals into another realm. I can't take you or the vampire, though. It's against the rules to portal demon carriers."

"You know Siobhan's alive?"

We trudged through the forest, pine needles and small branches snapping with each step.

"Yeah, and strong. She's not injured or anything too badly. I can feel it. You want me to take the girls to safety?"

"Yes," I said. "Please."

"What's your name, by the way?" the girl asked. "Corwin, was it?"

"Corban," I said. "The vampire girl is Liana. The ferrum worker is Gina, and the anthropologist is Amy."

"I'm Aline."

"Good to meet you," I said.

She barked a short laugh.

"Yeah," I said, "I wish the circumstances were better."

"Can you keep these weapons out of that guy's hands? The fallen guy?"

"I should be able to, yeah. Other angels will be converging here to fight him." The thing about my kind, when we fell, it wasn't a quiet event. Others would be on notice. "I'll get these weapons into their hands. I really hope you won't regret bringing them to us."

"Yeah, this is messed up. So messed up." She gave me a furtive, frightened glance. "It's my fault, isn't it?"

"What? No. No way. This is not your fault."

"We're told to stay away from your kind. I thought it was just to keep our secret, but I messed up. I told you stuff and that one guy couldn't take it."

"Aline," I said, "there is way more going on than you telling us how the world works. *Way* more, okay? It was a powder keg situation already. It's a good thing you were here, a miraculously good thing. Focus on saving Gina and Amy."

Another furtive glance; a coyote twitch in a human girl. "This isn't the end of the world, is it?"

"I hope not. I hope it's not even another angel war, but this is my kind's battle. We'll fix this, okay?"

The girl didn't look convinced, and I couldn't blame her. "Well…" she said, "there's more. That vampire you were running from? She's on her way here."

TWENTY-SIX

"So you can track all vampires?" I asked.

"I can feel them," said Aline. She bent her steps off to the right and I followed. We were nearing the cave, as best as I could tell. I'd had enough centuries of experience tracking and camping out in the woods to be able to navigate well, but it was always difficult when the world around me was changing. A steady stream of ash had begun to fall now, turning the once lush forest into an apocalyptic wasteland. Still, the incline of the ground under my feet and the amount of distance we'd covered put us near the cave. It should have been just ahead.

"Feel them how?" I asked.

"Like… because you guys have these spirits that are tethered to the demon realm, I can feel that there's, like, a string spanning the two places. Your kind I can sense, but there are always a zillion of you. Like, vampires are easier because usually there's not, like, a lot and the bond is different. 'Cept right now, there are a few hundred down in that town. What's it called? Toe-az?"

"Taos," I said, my heart sinking. Melanie was likely planning to sweep Taos to find Cassie the same way she'd swept Southampton to find Liana's house. How, I wondered, had she tracked us here? Perhaps we should have changed cars a few times in our trek out from New York.

"There's one of your kind with the vampire who's coming here."

There was an angel with Melanie? Odds were it was a hitch-hiker, staying hidden, but they would not want to be driven straight into a confrontation with one of the fallen. "Right," I said, "I should go intercept them. Where are they?"

"Getting close. You can probably meet them on the road if you run." Aline pointed off through the trees.

"Okay… I'll be right back then." I dropped the two bags of ferrum and headed off through the trees, running as fast as I could, cursing how underprepared I felt. I wasn't planning ahead, just running around in a desperate attempt to stay atop of a rapidly changing situation.

Now that the destruction had died down a little—there were no more lightning strikes, just the smell of the world burning and lots of ash—I realized how hungry I was. Blotches were swimming in my vision and I felt like I'd faint.

Amazingly, though, I did not feel like I wanted to hurt anyone and scarf down their suffering. I was craving food instead. Perhaps seeing Otuo fall had knocked some sense into me?

Up ahead I could see the road like a thin grey ribbon through the trees and I put on another burst of speed to jump out onto it.

Aline had been right. As soon as I emerged, there came a small motorcade of cars. First a sedan, followed by an SUV and behind that a large, RV-shaped vehicle.

In the space of two breaths they were speeding past me with a great whoosh of momentum, kicking up a great cloud of ash and dust. I couldn't run as fast as they drove, of course, but I ran anyway, hoping that the angel with them would see me and give some kind of sign.

The RV's door flew open and a figure hurled itself out, landing with a practiced tuck and roll.

Mouse.

Oh no, I thought.

Mouse got to her feet and brushed herself off as the group of cars cruised into the distance. She still wore her camouflaged t-shirt and cargo pants. I never knew if she did that so as to be able to hide from our own kind, or because it kept her in the right headspace to stealth around.

"Corban," she said. "You're alive."

"Where's Cassie?" I asked.

"With them." She pointed after the cars. "Melanie set her goons on us as we were on our way out of town. Then this fireworks show happened and... please tell me it wasn't Otuo?"

"Did you know he was about to fall?" I asked.

Rather than answer, she shut her eyes and looked for a moment like she might collapse. "I haven't been agreeing with him lately," she said. "He's been sticking to the rules a little too much, if that makes sense? Using them to justify spiritually questionable things?"

"Yeah, I get what you mean," I said. "Siobhan left the order—"

"She left the order?"

"And told me a bunch of secrets of the inner circle."

Mouse frowned. "You shouldn't have told me she was in the inner circle."

I was definitely out of it. This was a basic rule, and I'd blanked on it. "Sorry."

"Well, it doesn't really matter. I'm in the inner circle, too."

I shook my head, doing my best not to smirk at her. This wasn't a laughing matter, but given I didn't know what else to do, my urge was to laugh. "I can't tell you the whole story, but suffice it to say that Otuo got so furious, he fell. Come on." I started back down into the woods. "Liana's safe, for now. Her friends are, too."

"Her friends?"

It would take several minutes to walk back to where I'd left Aline. "I need to fill you in," I said.

ALINE WAS WAITING for us, in human form, which was good. I hadn't mentioned she was a shifter, only that she was a friend who'd helped us out.

She'd revealed herself to me and Siobhan and the girls, but that didn't mean she'd want to reveal herself to Mouse. Otuo also knew about her, and for the first time the significance of that hit me. The coyotes' secret was out. He had no reason to keep it for them. It might soon be open season on her kind.

"Aline," I said, "this is Inioluwa. We call her Mouse."

Mouse rushed forward before Aline could react and grasped her by the shoulders, staring keenly at her unusually pale brows.

"Hey…" I said. "Manners."

But Mouse had already let her go. "You're one of them."

"Look, Aline," I said. "I didn't tell her anything. We've already betrayed you in the worst way. Otuo could set out to destroy your people—"

"He could try," she said. "And that's not your fault. It was my decision to open my mouth. You trust her?" She jerked her head towards Mouse.

"Um, yeah, but—"

"Then we tell her."

At my baffled look, she added, "The people you like all seem to do the right thing. It was the guy you weren't sure about who fell. If you think she can be, like, trusted, then that's good enough for me. That angel fighting the fallen? Can I just say she's, like, totally amazing?"

"She is," I agreed. I picked up one of the duffel bags I'd dropped and gestured for Mouse to get the other one. She unzipped it and poked her hand in before I could say, "Careful!"

Too late. She jerked back with a hiss. "Ferrum?"

"Yes, we managed to keep these away from Otuo."

She looked at the weapons inside. "Corban, these daggers have blades twice the width of ours."

So they did. "They're old," I said.

"Old? They're from before we cut ties to the ferrum workers. There aren't any weapons from that era left," she protested. "They were all melted down."

"It's from a stash," said Aline. "A really old one. Let's, like, get walking. I'll explain stuff."

MOUSE WAS QUIETER than usual as we stepped up to the dark cave mouth, which I now noted was really small. I was amazed that I'd managed to squeeze in there.

"Liana?" I said.

Rustling noises, followed by Liana sticking her head out. Her face was grimy and her elbows caked in dirt. "You made it…" At the sight of Mouse she scrabbled the rest of the way out and got to her feet. Her clothes were filthy, and looking down, I saw I had a lot of dirt on my hands, and my jeans were coated in damp mud, which was coated in ash. Somehow Aline had avoided getting filthy; I wondered if shifting somehow shed the extra dirt. Strange how she could shift with her clothing on.

"My aunt?" Liana asked.

"Melanie's got her," said Mouse. "I'm sorry. They're taking her up to the ski valley—"

"Into a war zone?" Liana wrung her hands.

"Melanie herself is with them," I said. "She may be able to take down Otuo."

Mouse shot me a puzzled look. "Melanie herself wouldn't be so stupid. She always uses decoys. I'm sure the person leading that caravan is a decoy."

"No, the old vampire's there," said Aline. "I can tell."

"And she's too smart," I said, "to drive right into danger like that unless she's got a plan."

Liana was still distraught. "But my aunt—"

I held up my hands. "We'll do everything we can, okay? Everything."

By now Gina and Amy were also out of the cave. "You two," I said, "go with Aline. She'll take you somewhere safe."

"Somewhere where they might age forty years in five minutes?" Liana asked.

Gina and Amy exchanged a look, but it wasn't as baffled as I would have expected. Then again, what else would they have spent their time in that cave talking about? Liana had no doubt given them an in-depth briefing on all things supernatural.

Aline shook her head. "Time slippage happens in the portalling process for some others, but not us. Your friends'll stay the same age, same timeline, all that stuff."

"It's… sorry, kind of petty to care about that if this is the end of the world," Liana said.

"It's not the end of the world," said Mouse. "It's an angel war. We've survived them before. But yes, you two get to safety. Corban, we've got to get back down to Taos or to Santa Fe and rally troops to fight Otuo, and I need these weapons."

"Taos is crawling with vampires," I said. "So be careful."

Aline handed over her duffel bag without question.

I held onto mine, ready to set out with Mouse.

"No," said Liana. "If Melanie's here and distracted, we fight her. We free my aunt. If we wait, she'll have time to prepare and—"

"Don't be a fool," snapped Mouse. "Always have a plan before you attack. Don't run in blind."

"You remember what happened when I did that with Darissa?" I asked.

But tears were starting to streak down Liana's muddy cheeks. "I'm not leaving my aunt with her. I can't, okay? I just can't."

I handed my bag of weapons to Mouse. "Fine," I said. "We'll stay, scout things out, figure out what to do next."

"You're crazy," said Mouse. "Look at you. You're in no condition to fight."

"Just the two of us can stay under the radar," I said. "You go and rally troops. We've got some vehicles that aren't all that drivable, but are better than nothing."

She shook her head, but didn't argue.

TWENTY-SEVEN

"Y ou guys good to come with me?" Aline asked Amy and Gina.

The two looked at Liana before nodding.

"'Kay, so like, the best way to get somewhere safe is to walk this direction," Aline pointed. "It'll take about half a mile to get all the way across. It'll just look like the landscape is shifting around you."

I felt a twinge of jealousy. Were the circumstances any different, this sounded like a fun adventure.

Amy dug in her pocket and came up with the cell-phone looking device that had spooked me when I first saw it. She handed it to Liana. "I put some notes on there and stuff. The unlock code is J-A-C-K. I dunno if it can help you, but it's got all of the order's archives on it."

"All of them?" Liana asked.

"Well, everything on vampires and Nabateans," Amy amended. She gave Liana a fierce hug. "Be safe, okay?"

It was clear from Gina's pale complexion that she wasn't okay with splitting up and following a stranger to another world, but she was resolved. The logic of her universe had been thoroughly upended, and she had to follow the new logic where it went. She also gave Liana a fierce hug.

Neither she nor Amy looked at me or Mouse as they went to join Aline. We were already waning in their awareness. Liana, Mouse, and I watched as the trio took off walking through the woods. Their figures began to fade, until they looked ghostly and transparent.

Mouse gave a low whistle. "Quite the trick."

"I really hope this doesn't lead to the fallen angels hunting coyotes," I said. I knew in my bones that since Otuo had fallen, others would too. "I will feel personally responsible."

"Because you and Liana were who the coyotes trusted?" asked Mouse.

"Coyote," I said, "singular. I hope she doesn't get in trouble."

"Look Otuo didn't fall just because a coyote-girl got to him," said Mouse. "It was going to happen sooner or later." She pointed in the direction of the town, one eyebrow raised. I reoriented us towards where we'd ditched the vehicles and we all set out, Liana walking between and a step behind us. The footprints we'd made on our way to the cave were already filling in with more ash and Mouse looked like she'd been sprayed with the white flocking some people put on their Christmas trees. Liana was well on her way to sporting the same look.

"What made Otuo vulnerable?" I pressed. "What pushed him over the edge?"

"I'm not really sure, but I started noticing him struggle a few years ago. I caught him trying to ignore the pain of a group of people because they weren't religious."

"Uh, no..." I said. We did *not* call balls and strikes on religion. We all knew enough to realize that there was a whole lot we didn't know, and we didn't dictate what the truth was beyond our covenants and our beliefs in the supremacy of humans as moral beings.

"He didn't stay in tune with his humanity," came a husky voice with an Irish brogue from somewhere ahead of us in the haze.

My heart lifted, as Siobhan emerged from the woods. Gone were her stiletto heels—her feet were bare. Her pencil skirt was ripped and both sleeves of her blouse were gone, leaving only ragged hem.

Our footsteps in the ash had lasted long enough for her to follow, at least.

"Look who's doing the predictable thing," she said, "heading for the cars they salvaged." She closed the distance between us and clasped my hand briefly. This wasn't her being fresh. It was a way for me to tell she hadn't fallen. The fallen always sparked when they touched anyone else. Mouse grasped her hand and we all smiled in relief.

"He lost his compassion," she said. "He started justifying why certain people weren't worthy of it."

"It's true," Mouse agreed. "He started to get really literal about things, like that non-religious people couldn't be good."

"Ever?" I asked.

"And he was adamant that vampires are evil," said Siobhan, looking at Liana.

Who shrank into herself.

Siobhan gave her an apologetic smile. "I didn't know until I met up with him here, but something about you really upset him. I assumed it was that you violated the letter of the law, being a vampire, but now I wonder if it's that you were another tamer of demons?"

"Whoa, wait. Otuo sent me to help her," I said. "This doesn't make sense."

"To help her, or be destroyed by her?" Mouse asked. "And for the record, I didn't know either until we met up with Siobhan. Her saving Liana's friends just… set him off. Reuniting them with you was not okay with him."

"Why would he…" My mind spun. "Where is he now?" I asked.

"Asleep after gorging himself. I managed to herd all the humans out of town, except for one RV and some SUVs who won't listen. Seems a little vampire?"

I nodded. "It's Melanie."

"Well…" She sighed. "Thank heavens for that then, eh?"

"Why are you guys so sure that having Melanie go up against Otuo will be good?" Liana asked.

"Vampires have their uses," said Siobhan. "Doesn't serve their purposes to have modern civilization collapse."

"They helped save the eastern portion of the Roman Empire," I affirmed.

Siobhan nodded. "We end up allies of convenience at times like this, not that we won't still kill her when we get the chance. We've got limited time to go gather forces, though."

"They're not coming with us," said Mouse, pointing at me and Liana. "They're going after Cassie."

Siobhan didn't look as surprised as I would have expected. "How are you feeling?" she asked me.

"Starving," I admitted. The world had taken on a surreal, dreamlike quality, though the ash that was still softly raining down and the smell of burned homes and the fact that we could see no further than two or three trees deep in the forest factored in as well.

"You want my fear and pain?" Liana asked.

I considered that. I wanted to try fasting, but now was perhaps not the best time. "I don't want to take your feelings from you," I said.

"I'd actually like that. I know I got annoyed with you for doing it that time you helped me, years ago, in the alley, but you were right. They're a burden right before battle."

I looked at Mouse, who shook her head. "I was with Cassie the whole ride up here," she said. "I am stuffed."

Siobhan also held up her hands. "I was leaching off everyone Otuo was torturing."

"That a yes?" Liana asked.

I nodded, and felt her walls come down. One moment, the world was tranquil—our little corner of it, at least. The next I was hit with a deluge of terror, anger, frustration, and disappointment.

I drained down the terror first, which tasted like liquid chocolate dissolved into heavy cream. Then the frustration and the feelings of helplessness. Those were like a juicy steak, filling to someone who wasn't a ravenous, empty void. It didn't fill me, but I focused on how good it felt to imbibe and pushed away the hunger pangs that demanded more. The disappointment was next, and was like fresh baked bread. I could almost smell it in the air. The anger I looked to last. It reminded me of espresso, but I paused before touching it. Much of this, I knew, was anger at me. At my lies, and at the unfinished business between us. It didn't feel right to siphon that out of her when I'd been the original cause.

Liana looked over at me.

I took a deep breath and closed myself up, doing my best to ignore her emotional aura.

After a moment, she closed up her mind as well, and the air was clear again.

I felt a little stronger. That feeding had been a small drop in a deep ocean, but I was starting to remember what it was like to make do with small drops. I could endure a lot on very little.

It was a short walk to the road and the two cars, which looked derelict. Ash lay on them in a thick layer and when I took a swipe at one of the windows, it smeared. This would be a nightmare to clean up. Aline had given me her keys before leaving with the girls, so I offered both sets to Mouse. "Take your pick."

She ignored the keys and went to do a slow walk around each car, her soft-soled shoes soundless against the ash-covered asphalt. "The truck," she said, at last.

I handed her the Suburban keys. "It's missing a couple of tires," I said.

"Yeah, I saw that, but it's easier to drive on this kind of rims than what your car has. Might tear up the road some." She shrugged. "We'd best move now. I don't want to be anywhere near Melanie when she takes on Otuo."

Mouse climbed into the driver's seat and shut the door, raising a big cloud of ash that both Liana and I retreated from. I handed my bag of ferrum weapons to Siobhan, who jogged around to the passenger side and got in, pausing to wave with a simple flip of her wrist.

With a few chugs, the engine started and then the windshield wipers began to move, raising yet another cloud. Liana and I backed up to stand behind our rental car. "Corban, here," said Mouse, through her rolled-down window. She dug into one of the duffel bags and tossed some items out before taking off. The truck swerved unsteadily as the tire-less wheels tried to drag her off the road. In moments she'd disappeared into the cloudy haze. I squatted down to see what she'd tossed at me. Some leather lined cuffs and an extra dagger, one of the old fashioned kind. This one I could take into a fight and not worry about it snapping.

Liana stood over me, the ash in her hair and the dirt on her clothes making her look once more like an action movie heroine, right down to the flawless features. Vampy, but pretty just the same. There were even a few flakes of ash dusting her eyelashes.

"Can we talk?" I asked her. This wasn't the best time, I knew, but there wouldn't be any better times in the near future, and I'd put it off long enough.

The look she gave me wasn't pure venom.

TWENTY-EIGHT

If there was one constant in my time with Liana, it was that there was never a good time for the serious talks we needed to have. One or the other of us was always in the midst of some insane tragedy.

Liana knew this as well as I did and folded her arms.

"I'm sorry," I said. "I should have talked to you about my feelings before. It shouldn't have gone down that way."

She shrugged. "So I push you towards falling? Otuo thinks I'll destroy you? Let's just—"

"You don't," I said. "I was wrong, and it was petty of me to say. I guess even I'm not too old for heartbreak."

"What's that supposed to mean?"

"You're getting over me," I said. "And I should just let that happen. I shouldn't be selfish."

"There's no point liking each other," she countered. "It's not gonna happen, unless we get into weird kinky stuff like wearing full nylon bodysuits or something."

I paused to let that image sink in. "Pardon?"

"I'm not elaborating." Her hackles were well and truly raised.

For once, I was able to stifle the urge to laugh. It was clear, though the air remained devoid of emotion, that she was embarrassed, and as cute as it was to see her face flush deep red, it wasn't nice to revel in that right now. "Look," I said, "every time we have touched, it hasn't made me any worse. I wonder, actually, if it's made me better. I've had an easier time dealing with the dark hunger on this trip than makes sense. Sometime, when we're not likely to die in the next 24 hours…" I took a deep breath. I was about to say something deeply selfish. "I'd like to try touching again. Kissing you made me human, and there's a chance that it could happen again."

"Or you could die."

"Well, obviously if it looks like that's happening, we stop."

She turned her gaze away. "I can't. I'm sorry. I missed you when you were gone, but now… I miss life being normal and boring and dull. I mean, as much as it ever gets like that for me. I see people that no one else sees and I know that there are magic users portalling over from other worlds and fighting climate change, but that stuff aside, I liked having a normal life."

This was exactly what I should have wanted for her. Given that, I forced a nod, even as I felt like someone was taking scissors to my heart and snipping it into tiny, bloody pieces. To be this close to her and yet know that if I reached out to touch her cheek, I'd have my hand slapped away, was far worse than pining for her while leaping and climbing over the few permanent structures of a refugee camp as everyone else slept. Nevertheless, I said, "Okay."

I expected that to be the end of the conversation, but Liana didn't move, not even her gaze shifted. After a moment, she sighed. "It doesn't even seem right, you and me."

Rather than offer up reasons in support of that, I waited to hear hers.

"There's the age gap," she said.

"Sure, there is that."

"I tried to write up lists of why you and I were wrong for each other."

That was so very Liana.

"And?"

"And, I kept on finding reasons we might work. It was kind of pointless while I was still obsessed with you."

Was, I noted. She was speaking about her feelings for me in past tense.

"I mean," she went on, "there's the age gap, but I was noting down stuff like the fact that biologically you're not older than me, and that you haven't really lived a life up until now. You've just had this existence. You haven't been married or had kids or stuff. I have more romantic experience than you." Still she stared off into space.

Everything she said was true.

"I guess the thing I kept zeroing in on was that it's messed up for someone your age to look twice at someone who's my age."

Now it was my turn to look away. "Sure."

"I mean, why? Or is this normal for you, to fall for some mouthy, independent girl and try to get her to ascend?"

"What?" I asked.

"You know, Siobhan, Mouse."

"Um… there was never anything romantic there," I said. Though now that she mentioned it, she was right that I did have a habit of turning mouthy, brave, independent women. Well, Mouse wasn't particularly talkative, but the way she moved through the world demonstrated defiance.

"Okay." Liana shrugged.

It was a natural endpoint of the conversation, but I couldn't let it go. "Liana, I haven't felt this way about anyone, ever. And I shouldn't be saying this or digging in… The thing is, though, I really care about you."

"You care about everyone."

"Not like this, okay? I'm sorry, this is totally wrong of me—"

"Then stop," she cut me off, fixing me with a direct stare. "Don't do it." And with that, she started heading into town.

I stayed on her heels. "Liana—"

"What?" She spun around and faced me. "What are you trying to say?"

What *was* I trying to say? That I had a selfish desire to make her mine? That I fantasized about kissing her so often that it was where my mind went whenever it had a break? That all the progress she'd made towards putting me behind her was killing me? "I don't know," I said. "I'm sorry."

"You don't have to be sorry. It's… flattering. I guess."

You guess… I did my best to absorb the sting without having it show. "Sorry if I seem like a dirty old man or something."

"You seem like a sweet, soft-hearted guy who has a bad habit of taking on more than you can handle."

"Hey, I've been able to handle things just fine for two thousand years."

"Until now, when you're on the brink of falling—"

"I'm not on the brink. Yeah, I've been unsteady, but I can handle it." As I said the words, I realized they were true. So what if life was more of a struggle now than it had been before? I could struggle. I had centuries of practice, keeping myself grounded.

"Well, good." Liana's words fell flat and even she seemed to feel it. "Moving on… How do vampires kill fallen angels, then? How does anyone?"

With effort, I redirected my attention to the new topic. "A touch is still deadly for a fallen angel," I said. "Decapitation works. Electrocution works."

"Electrocution? He's throwing freaking lightning bolts."

"Yeah… I don't know the physics, but hitting the fallen with live power lines takes them down. That's why you can bet the power is out here in town."

"I was kind of hoping to be able to watch the news."

"Me too," I said. "But without a battery operated television, I don't know how. Let's go find Melanie and your aunt. Let's go see if they've found Otuo." I walked with a purpose towards town, aware that the scent of char was getting more pungent and there was a soft glow up ahead that was likely buildings on fire.

"What about your phone?" Liana asked.

I paused. "Yeah, okay, I can look up the news on that, but we assume Melanie can track it. Actually, we know Otuo can. He knew we'd shielded it."

"Oh… right." Liana's stomach growled, loud enough that she pressed a hand to it in embarrassment.

She hadn't eaten in hours, I realized. The sandwiches Siobhan promised to get for the group had never materialized, and we'd done a madcap dash into the woods and a leisurely walk out in the meantime.

"Food for you next," I said. "Let's go see if the convenience store is still intact." I shut my eyes, trying to remember the right direction to walk.

"Can I just make a request?"

"Mmm-hmm," I said.

"Can you not eat a ton of junk? I mean, I get that it doesn't matter, but seriously, it's a bad habit and I'm stressed out and I can't just roll with your bad habits right now. If you ever are human again, you'll only live, like, ten years, the way you eat."

So we weren't together, but I still got criticized? Rather than feel annoyed, my hopeless heart clung to the fact that she'd mentioned me becoming human again. I pinpointed the direction to the convenience store, and with a nod, headed off.

LUCK WAS WITH us. The convenience store was intact, save for some soot built up on the windows and a fire burning across the street. Most of that building had been consumed, though, so the heat billowing off it wasn't skin-peeling.

Liana seemed a little put-off by me opening the door and striding in, but her mood shifted as I pulled a couple of hundreds out of my wallet and put them in the locked cash register. Odds were they'd burn along with the rest of the building eventually, but just in case…

Together we went up and down the aisles. Liana grabbing a loaf of bread and some cold cuts and cheese to make herself a sandwich.

I mimicked her, making one as well—I hadn't had thin-sliced meat or cheese in centuries.

So I was surprised how good the sandwich tasted. I hadn't remembered liking food much when I was mortal, though there was a good chance that I was carting around memory fragments of whatever I'd eaten while a soldier. I didn't remember what that was, specifically, but it left an icky residue in my mind.

Liana wolfed down her sandwich, swigging bottled water between bites, while I reached out to see if I could tell where Melanie's caravan had gone. We hadn't seen the slightest hint of it so far, and I wasn't surprised that I felt no hint of it now.

Any humans with Melanie would have been trained to wall their minds.

Well, all except for Cassie, of course. I wondered if they'd drugged her, or if they were just too far away for me to sense her.

Once done eating, Liana went back to foraging, taking things off the shelves and checking the prices.

Of course she checked the prices.

"Okay," she said. "I think I'm all set. Let's go."

TWENTY-NINE

We managed to find tire tracks in the ash, and followed them uphill deeper into town, until we came upon the hulk of the RV, with a few SUVs parked around it. They all seemed empty.

"Right," Liana said. "Find a place to hide me, and I'll wrap up in my space blanket so no one can see my infrared signature, while you go through the vehicles to find my aunt."

She was such a forward-thinking nerd.

The buildings around here looked like they'd been blasted rather than burned, so there were still some standing walls. It was a simple matter of finding a nice, secure corner that didn't have any exposed electrical wires or other dangers. Once we'd located such a place and Liana had the space blanket wrapped securely over her, I headed for the vehicles.

They were as abandoned as they had looked on approach. The SUVs were only slightly modified with a blackout area behind the front seats where vampires could ride—and evidently had, judging by the distinctive smell they left. Cassie had been confined to one of these too—the physical stink of her fear was unmistakeable, and yet I still couldn't taste her emotions in the ether. How far away was she and how had they moved her so fast?

The RV was a strange control center of sorts with screens that looked like radar and sonar readouts, plus the predictable infrared. I checked that to make sure Liana wasn't visible. Knowing where to look, I saw the small heat signature of her breath, venting from under the blanket.

At the back of the RV was another blackout area—a cubicle made of opaque material that ensured no sunlight would penetrate. The rest of the vehicle was windowless, but this area would stay dark even when the RV door was open. It had no discernible door of its own.

Many might have been fooled, but I was old and I'd seen many a trick in my lifetime. There would be a door, one with the latch on the inside. Melanie would have a key that would activate an electromagnet to lift the latch. Hence, I could find the door if I could find the scratches left by the key. They were usually fine and faint. I had to run my fingers over each wall until I finally found the slight scrapes and the mildest discoloration.

Melanie might have had many, many years in this world, but she still couldn't discover all the secrets about my kind. Tracing my finger along the key marks, I felt the latch give and the door swung open. No lock worked against an angel. It was a simple rule of the universe.

Inside was a reclining couch and silken throw, a wall screen television, and a minibar. Despite the small space, it provided palatial luxury, and the scent here was distinctly vampire.

Melanie's own room.

As nice as it was, it seemed small. Then again, the RV was ostentatious enough. She didn't want to draw the eye of human authority figures.

Overall, the setup spoke of someone with a lot of money and access to technology. This vehicle appeared to have been custom made from the chassis on up, and I wasn't aware of many assembly plants that did that. The twenty-first century was modular. It was rare for humans to have anything completely custom made; those were more often relics of bygone ages. Everything from clothing to cars to computers to houses tended to be designed in bulk nowadays.

There wasn't much else to learn, so it was with a measure of frustration that I opened the door back into the main cabin, then went to exit the RV, and found myself face to face with a vampire.

A row of vampires, that was. This meant two things. One was that the sun had set. The other was that Melanie had instructed her minions to stand just outside the door, no doubt thinking she could trap me, or whichever angel came snooping, in. I made myself take a few deep breaths. Despite the open door and lights from the interior washing over these minions, they didn't react. They couldn't see me and didn't know the door was open.

Vampires also stood in a tight ring around each of the SUVs, and presumably the sedan, too, though I couldn't see that from my vantage point. I forced myself to calm down and think. How had they known when to surround the vehicles?

Liana. Had they found her? Slight as her physical signs were, she was the one detectible physical presence that could alert Melanie that someone was near.

I jumped and grabbed the top of the doorway in one hand, then gritted my teeth as I hauled myself up and onto the roof, the metal from the doorway digging hard into my palms.

There was no one on the roof, which was either an oversight or another layer of trap. I suspected the former. Most angels couldn't perform the kind of acrobatics I did. The top of the RV was smooth, but flat, which enabled me to reach over the edge and pull the door shut. Had she modified an Airstream, I probably wouldn't have been able to get the door shut without sliding off the arched roof, and if I left the door open, the vamps might eventually catch on that someone had been there, and my cover would be partially blown.

Standing up as tall as I could, I peered off in Liana's direction. Was she still there? Still safe? If Melanie had located her, then going to help her definitely meant going into a trap.

Normally that would mean I had to do anything but go rescue Liana, but my current situation was more like my situation way back when I was in the Roman army. I wasn't in charge of taking down Melanie or Otuo. In the grand war, I was no more than a foot soldier. My duty was to protect Liana and any reconnaissance I did might help Siobhan and Mouse, but they didn't expect it of me.

I went to the far end of the roof and took a running leap off the top of the RV, jumping well clear of the SUVs and landing with a drop roll a few paces away from the structure where I'd hidden Liana.

There was no one in the structure, as far as I could see. As I peered around the broken edge of the wall, I saw the shapeless lump that was Liana's hiding place in the still-intact corner— she'd dusted her mylar blanket with ash to cut down on the shine, and it worked well as camouflage. I made my way over to her.

"Hey," I whispered.

She was so still it was as if she'd been turned to stone.

"It's me." I peeled back a corner of the blanket. "I think they found you, so we'd better get away from here, fast."

Her wide, scared eyes gazed at me from the darkness, then she got moving, shaking out the blanket and folding it away with cold efficiency into the bag with the other items from the convenience store, which she tucked under one arm.

"We assume," I said, "that Melanie has some kind of booby trap to detect our presence. Those rarely work, but she gets lucky sometimes. We need to get out of here without activating any kind of tripwire or anything like that. Get on my back."

Liana paused, blinking at me. "Pardon?"

"Get on my back. I'm going to climb out of here." I turned my back on her for emphasis, stooping so that she could climb on.

After a moment, she did, jumping so that I could grasp her behind the knees while she wrapped her arms around my neck. The bag from the convenience store thudded against my side, which would be awkward, but I could manage it. "I haven't done this since I was four," she said.

"Hang on." I bent my knees, then made a standing jump onto the broken wall and ran its length, leaping off the end and sailing into the street. Then I set her down, just as someone blew a whistle behind us.

Floodlights switched on, illuminating the area around the vehicles, and vamps and humans came boiling out of the wrecked buildings, dark shadowy figures in the dusk moving with military precision to make a ring around us and the vehicles. There weren't enough to create a complete cordon, which to me meant they had some other mechanism for sweeping the area or blocking us in.

Liana's whole body tensed. I'd put my arm around her to keep her protected and invisible.

"What's going on?" she whispered.

"They knew where you were, I guess, and once you disappeared from there, they knew that an angel had rescued you, which means they know that you and an angel are still somewhere nearby." That was impressive work for a vampire and her minions.

"So let's run." She pointed to a gap between two vampires.

It did look like plenty of room to slip through. I held up my hand, palm forward, and began to walk, my other arm firmly around Liana's waist. She didn't protest as I held her close to my side.

Slowly and steadily we approached the gap, and the vampires didn't react. As we got closer, I held my breath. Still no reaction.

They stood still in the eerie, ashen gloom. I could feel Liana's heart pounding, I held her so close.

As we came ever closer, I sensed something was very, very wrong. Melanie wasn't stupid enough to have her minions just stand there, looking intimidating, while one of my kind waltzed away. I took a deep breath and detected the faintest scent of ozone.

I stopped walking.

Liana looked up at me, eyes questioning. She didn't dare talk to me while we were this close.

I shut my eyes. The ozone could have been from the lightning strikes when Otuo fell, but what if it wasn't? There was a very, very rare and hard to generate barrier that zapped my kind badly. Not badly enough to kill us unless we were weakened, but still. A spark like that could hurt or kill Liana, and would definitely give away our location. It was almost unheard of to find one of these barriers on Earth and they required a high order magic user to make the machinery that powered them.

But Melanie might well have procured such machinery. It would only work for three nights, but that felt like an eternity right now.

Liana put her hand on my shoulder, gaze still questioning.

I leaned forward onto the balls of my feet and felt the tingle that made me pull back, turn us around and walk us towards the vehicles. Whether or not Melanie had actually procured a field to contain me or just faked up the signs of one, I knew I couldn't risk trying to walk away. I'd been outplayed.

THIRTY

"What are you doing?" Liana asked as I found a spot atop a small section of intact roof that was within the ring of captors and had a good view of the vehicles.

Of course, this made it an obvious place for me to take shelter. Melanie would be able to guess I was here, though I'd avoided three places with better views, including one with some shelter from the wind behind the lip of a parapet. At least she'd have to do some hunting to locate us.

"I don't trust that they'd let us go like that," I said. "It's got to be a trap."

"What kind of trap?"

I explained my knowledge of magical barriers, and added, "Or she's got something else to use against us. I just know that if I'm fighting someone like Melanie and something looks too good to be true, it's a trap."

"You sure that isn't the trap?" Liana asked. "You thinking that we're trapped?"

"Maybe," I said. "But I'm not going to test it."

Liana shrugged, her shoulder sliding against my chest. "Yeah, okay."

I shifted so I could look her in the eye. "I'm also not sure how well my powers will work the longer I go without feeding."

"You can feed off me. I've got plenty of fear and anger and stuff."

"Yeah, about that…"

She lifted an eyebrow.

"Come out, come out wherever you are," sang a feminine voice that sent an icy stab through my heart.

Liana tapped me on the chest and pointed.

A young woman with long, dark hair stood in the road off to our left. She was wearing skintight clothing—skinny jeans and a form fitting top.

"Is that Melanie?" Liana whispered.

"It could be," I said, "but it's hard to tell from here. She does look like that, yeah."

The woman looked around, intently. I braced myself, focused on her. Then Otuo stepped out into the road.

Oh… The lightbulb went on in my mind. Getting a magical barrier to trap me seemed like overkill, but to trap Otuo? That made sense. Melanie might have had the equipment to make the barrier with her for centuries, waiting for a chance like this. I had no idea how she'd baited him; I'd been too busy worrying about Liana.

I let myself relax. "Well, at least she'll take care of him."

"You sure about that?" Liana asked.

"Melanie doesn't pick fights she can't win. If that's her, then she's got a lock. Even if it isn't her—and it probably isn't. It's probably a decoy. Even so, she's got a plan to take him down."

Liana squirmed and I loosened my grip on her. "Sorry," I said.

"You're fine. Thanks for keeping me alive and hidden and stuff." There might have been a hint of humor in her voice, but I didn't dare hope for that. Liana was fair in her judgment and good tempered, but me holding her this close would test the fairness and good temperament of anyone. "Your body is seriously cold, though," she added.

I focused on Otuo.

My old mentor looked worse for wear. He was barefoot now, his jeans ragged and torn at the knees, his shirt gone. His skin was ashen—literally. Particles of ash clung to it in a fine layer, giving him the look of carved, dulled stone. The floodlights made him look washed out and corpselike.

I had never seen a vampire take down a fallen angel. Few of my kind had. Whenever a fight this epic was about to go down, sensible members of my kind went for cover. I wondered if I should do that, if whatever Melanie was about to use on Otuo might take me out as well. There was also the fact that Otuo could see me, if he looked in the right direction. We were laying low and in the darkness, but given I was used to being invisible to enemies, I felt like I might as well have had a large arrow floating in the air, pointing down at me.

But Liana was riveted on the scene unfolding before us, and I had to confess I was too. Our odds of surviving this night were slim to none anyway, so perhaps we ought to enjoy as much of the show as we could.

My mind rejected this, though. I couldn't just sit idly by and help bring about my beloved's demise. "We should go," I whispered to her. "Find shelter. Whatever happens next could be really destructive."

"Then we need to stay up here," Liana countered. "We don't want to huddle somewhere a wall might collapse on us."

"I've heard that fallen angels can emit a blinding light that burns my kind and humans to ash," I said.

"You think that's what all this ash is?" Liana asked, running a finger across the tarred roof beneath our feet. "Gross."

"It's just that—"

"Yeah, I heard you." She didn't move.

I don't know if she would have resisted me trying to make her move, but I didn't try. Perhaps the fight had gone out of me. Perhaps I trusted her judgment implicitly. Perhaps I was in so far over my head that I was paralyzed with fear.

Otuo and the woman who might have been Melanie stood in the road. He stared at her, then finally cleared his throat, letting her see him.

Her entire focus snapped to him. "Do you remember me?" Melanie asked.

"You came yourself?" Otuo croaked. "Should I be flattered? Or do you think you alone can stand against me?"

Her lips curved up into a cruel smile of triumph. "I have a proposition. Let's not fight, you and I. Let's not waste valuable time and energy battling each other."

"And do what instead? Join forces? I have no interest in working with you or anyone else. I have a job to do."

"Punishing humanity for its sins? Scourging the Earth?"

"Something like that."

"Something I have no patience for," the vampire replied. She held up a hand, though. "But we have a common enemy to flush out right now. Corban Alexander and his vampire lover. Strange that you fell and he didn't... I'm at a distinct disadvantage, hunting him. You are not."

"They're long gone from here," said Otuo.

"They are within a hundred yards of us right this very minute. You see, I have the girl's aunt. They are likely watching and listening to everything we say."

Otuo's frame straightened and he began to cast his gaze around.

"Don't move," I whispered to Liana. "Freeze. Like stone." Movement would attract the eye.

My old mentor's head swiveled in our direction and I felt the piercing power of his gaze on us.

Well done, I thought. It'd been less than an hour since I'd moved to scope out Melanie's operation, and I'd managed to get us captured and killed. After two thousand years, I would have hoped I could make it a day at least.

But Otuo's gaze didn't linger or even pause. He turned away, scanning other rooftops.

"Do you think he saw us?" Liana whispered.

"I don't think he did."

"Or is he protecting us?"

"He's not," I said. "He wouldn't. Not while he's like this. He didn't see us."

"So—"

"If those two are actually forming an alliance," I interrupted, "she can use him to hunt down all of my kind."

"Oh, right, that's bad…"

I felt sick to my stomach, as if the food I'd eaten had begun to rot inside me. Here I'd thought that Melanie might form a loose alliance with us to deal with Otuo. Never had I heard of a vampire teaming up with one of the fallen to hunt my kind. The persistent animosity between our races had been one of the foundational rules of my universe, and like so many others, it was crumbling to dust before my eyes. Siobhan and Mouse and their allies were in serious trouble.

"Do you have surveillance video of the area?" Otuo asked Melanie.

"I do, yes."

"Fine, let me see it."

"Okay," said Liana. "Don't make a sound. If you get yourself killed, I'll never speak to you again."

I flicked my gaze in her direction, but she moved too fast for me to stop her. Before full dread could even build in my chest, she'd torn away from me and was off and running.

THIRTY-ONE

I wanted to go after Liana as she leapt off the edge of the roof and landed with a drop-roll behind a section of broken wall. I wanted to cover her, protect her, but I couldn't. Otuo was scanning the roofline and if I moved, I was dead, and then there would be no one to protect her.

Not that I knew how anyone was going to do that now. I couldn't even see Liana anymore, only hear her. She sounded like she was scuffling with someone. A vampire, no doubt, a bloodsucker about to dig its fangs into her neck.

"Corban," she snapped, startling me. "Let me go!" More scuffling, and then I caught a flash of her pale cheek as she bolted between buildings.

Melanie and Otuo reacted at once with shouts, and the vampire minions who had begun to mill around and go glassy-eyed in their posts now rallied to action. They closed in on Liana—making it obvious where she was as they shifted to track her movements. She was running right for Melanie, turning only to avoid debris and walls and vamps who dove at her.

And yet, even in my shock and fear, I noted that she ran at human speed. Here she was, charging at a major vampire boss, dodging her minions, and not turning fully vampire herself.

"Wait!" Liana shouted, leaping into the road where Melanie and Otuo stood. She had her hands up. "If either of you ever want to see Gamlat again, wait."

No, I thought. What was she doing?

And yet, Melanie held up a hand, stilling her minions while Liana kept her arms raised in surrender. All I could see from my vantage point was her back, and I couldn't read from her stance whether she was confident or scared, winging it or scheming.

Otuo just stared, eyes wide, as if Liana had offered him a one way ticket to paradise.

Otuo and… Gamlat? Had a history? How would Liana know that?

Regardless of how she'd figured it out, her knowledge wouldn't protect her for long. She was facing off against another Nabatean vampire by herself while I was close enough to watch but too far to help. That was a scene I had never, ever wanted to repeat. My fingers clenched, digging into the tar of the roof beneath me. I could throw my daggers, but even if I got perfect hits, I'd only take out two vamps, and Otuo would see me, and that would be that.

"I know the truth," said Liana. "I know that Gamlat's in the demon realm."

Those words hit like the bolts of lightning that had come rocketing down earlier. *Was* Gamlat in the demon realm? How would Liana know?

The data drive. It was still in the bag from the convenience store, which Liana had left with me. I had to take care not to disturb it. If it rustled, Otuo might overhear. Amy had written up her conclusions about the portal to the demon realm being in Petra. Gamlat had always stayed near Petra. If she'd ever managed to open that portal, there could be evidence of that. My kind just hadn't known where to look.

"Your brothel," said Liana. "The one in Boston. I know about that. I know you were breeding humans to make the perfect host to re-summon your sister. You kept turning the subjects, but none of them brought Gamlat back from the demon realm."

I clenched my teeth while I examined her theory for holes. It was true that the brothel had existed after Gamlat's disappearance, and that Melanie had been breeding humans and turning them. Could that really be what she was doing? Trying to get a human with the right characteristics to summon Gamlat's spirit from the demon realm? Had Liana figured out, after one coyote-shifter's crash course in parallel worlds, one of the strangest mysteries the order had never solved?

Melanie was too cunning to give anything away, though, and Liana was well out on a limb at this point. The old vampire inclined her head, as if amused.

"Your sister was trying to bring Gamlat back, too," said Liana. "Did you know that?"

Now she was going farther out on that limb, and I could hear it metaphorically cracking. Darissa had been a researcher like her sister, but spent most of her time wreaking havoc on the order and toying with humans. If Melanie was the studious, bespectacled sibling who stayed up late on a Friday night to finish homework, Darissa had been the willful teenager climbing out of her bedroom window and partying until sunrise.

Melanie, however, stood up straighter. She said nothing, asked nothing, only stared.

So Liana kept talking. "You know what she did when she held me prisoner? She tested me. You want to know the results?"

"You're going to tell me you're carrying Gamlat's soul," said Melanie. "That if I make you turn, I'll have her back."

"Not possible," said Otuo.

I knew Liana was lying now. Darissa had tested her to figure out how to make more daywalking vampires. Even if Liana's guess about Melanie's lab was correct, Melanie's notes and research from that era were so arcane, none of my kind nor humanity could decipher them. Liana was gambling the highest stakes gamble possible. If her guess was off by even a little, she was dead.

Well, she was already dead.

Even if she was correct about Gamlat being in the demon realm and the purpose of Melanie's lab, Melanie was ancient, wily, and skilled in negotiation. She lifted her chin, the only sign she gave that she was calculating her response. "What kind of test? A cheek swab?"

"Among other tests."

"What other tests?"

"I'm not sure," said Liana. "I only know the results."

"Do you now?"

"Yeah. We found them in the lab of the urgent care center. That's where she brought me to be tested."

Liana, my heart pleaded with her to stop this mad game. Melanie had and would always have the upper hand. I was stuck, unable to intervene, while Melanie toyed with my beloved the way a cat toyed with a mouse it had caught and could easily kill. Liana's continued prevarications were the panicked squeaks of a prey animal running out of seconds.

"And," said Melanie, "you are going to say the results claim that you are carrying my sister."

"Well, they match your notes," said Liana.

Ah… there was that. Melanie knew we had her notes. Liana hadn't overplayed her hand quite yet, but she would any second.

Otuo took a step closer to her, his gaze full of regret and longing.

The vampire tossed her head. "What are the odds that you, of all people, would be the one person that I must keep alive to save Gamlat?"

"Doesn't matter," said Liana. "All I need to know are the odds that you aren't going to risk losing her."

Stop, I wanted to scream. *You can't win this Liana.* Brilliant as she was, she was outgunned and being outmaneuvered. I could all but see Melanie setting up to flank her, a pincer move that would take Liana down.

But Liana wouldn't stop. "You're not going to risk losing your one shot at getting her back. Not after losing Darissa. Gamlat's like both a sister and mother to you. She misses you too, did you know that?"

Melanie froze. It was only for a fraction of a second, but I saw it, like a hitch in a film projection.

Liana saw it too. "I sense her sometimes, you know? I feel some of her feelings."

"You lie," said Melanie. "You know nothing of her feelings. She probably doesn't even miss me."

"I know that I, a mere human with very little life experience, was able to kill Darissa easily. I let myself turn right before I did it, though, so it wasn't really me doing it, was it? Perhaps it was someone eager to summon Darissa back to the demon realm." Liana folded her arms.

I hoped and prayed—prayed to any supernatural force that might listen—that she could be devious enough, talk fast enough, and catch enough lucky breaks to survive this gambit.

"You trying to convince me to kill myself to rejoin my sisters?" Melanie asked. "Nice try. Death doesn't send a soul to the demon realm."

Why-oh-why did Liana have to be so rash? Had her confidence overpowered her good sense? Was she desperate to protect me?

Yes, came the answer to my mind. There was only one thing that would push Liana Linacre to act rashly. It was the only reason she'd run towards the fight when everyone else had run away. She rushed in where my kind feared to tread because she put other people before herself. First it was her Aunt Cassie, and now it was me.

My mind spun like a top that had already started to wobble but wouldn't fall down. I couldn't see a way out, but my thoughts raced anyway, probing the contours of the situation, looking for a loophole or a back door.

Melanie made a show of sighing. Vampires didn't have to breathe. "Take her prisoner," she said. "Congratulations, girl, you've bought yourself the time it takes for me to run my own tests. Enjoy the last twenty minutes of your life."

Liana didn't move or struggle as two vamps closed in on her and bound her hands behind her back.

Belatedly, I realized that I had exactly five seconds to make a move, or else Liana's sacrifice would be for naught and I'd be in the worst position possible.

THIRTY-TWO

I slipped down off the roof, wishing I had the benefit of Mouse's dark skin. She could blend in with the night, while my skin reflected any light source, no matter how dim.

Otuo was still watching Liana, frozen as if stunned. He'd never been a soldier and warrior per se, but at his age he'd fought enough battles to know the importance of watching his back.

I could move fast or quietly, but not both. I chose fast, since Melanie was already turning to walk Liana towards the RV.

Otuo heard me and began to turn, but I anticipated that. I had my dagger out and focused on a spot by his breastbone. He had only enough time to rear back slightly before I was upon him, blade slipping between his ribs.

"Corban, stop!" Liana screamed.

It was too late. With a soft popping noise and a shower of dust, my ancient mentor was gone. Killed by my own hand.

I didn't have time to mourn, only to sheath my dagger and disappear back into the broken buildings. Experience told me that Melanie would pounce on me the second after seeing me kill Otuo, but she didn't. As I got my bearings, I saw that she and everyone else in the pool of light were looking the wrong direction.

Liana had her back to me, and it heaved with sobs. Terror and anxiety poured from her, saturating the air.

She'd miscued them, just like she'd done when pretending to fight with me before running out into the open. Because Melanie knew that Liana could see me, Liana knew that she could mislead Melanie and her minions about where I was.

As I watched, the vampire pulled herself up to her full height and turned around to look at where Otuo had been. "I see," she said. "Very clever." She snatched Liana by the back of her shirt and lifted until her toes barely touched the ground.

Liana didn't give her the satisfaction of a struggle, only stared back. A few stray tears coursed down her cheeks and her face reddened as she wasn't able to breathe. Her hands were still tied behind her back.

I bled away her fear and anxiety, imbibing it as fast as I could without losing control. Her expression didn't change.

"There will be more like Otuo on their way, you know?" said Melanie. "He's not the only one who's fallen."

Liana didn't reply.

"You can't protect your angel lover forever."

"He's not my lover." Liana choked out the words.

Melanie let go of her shirt and Liana fell to the ground, as if boneless. As she picked herself up, the rest of the vampires closed in on her, ready to hear what Melanie would do to her.

"Take her into the van," she said.

I couldn't see Liana as the crowd moved towards the RV. The door opened, then closed. The vampires who didn't go in formed a tight ring around the vehicle to prevent me getting inside.

I brushed the dust off myself and took a moment to let what had just happened sink in. Otuo, the oldest angel the world had ever known, was dead. I'd killed him. The founder of the order, the one person responsible for who and what I was, the one who'd helped me when I ascended and who'd been my mentor and my teacher... that supernatural entity was now dust. I hadn't even come to terms with him falling, yet.

I was reminded of Liana killing Darissa. It was such a monumental achievement, but it was over so fast. It had to be over fast. Fast was the only way to catch a being like that unawares.

Still, I wished I had a filmmaker's ability to play the scene in slow motion, and perhaps have a moment to monologue before and after. A soundtrack would have been nice too. Running, stabbing, and then brushing away the aftermath didn't satisfy me emotionally. It made my nerves jangle and my breathing ragged.

But I could breathe without worrying about being heard, now. I could walk out in the open again and stalk and fight the way I was used to. At least, I hoped that was true.

I pulled my phone out of the Faraday bag and called Siobhan.

"Otuo's dead," I said when she picked up.

"What? Really? Melanie killed him?"

"No… he was going to ally with her to hunt us, but Liana distracted him long enough that I was able to kill him. Apparently he and Gamlat… were lovers once?"

Siobhan was silent for a long time. "Lovers?" she asked. "Or was she his wife?"

"I don't know. I'm sorry I killed him before we could get answers," I said.

"No, you did what had to be done. And that's not really the issue right now…"

My stomach gave a lurch. "Others are falling?"

"They are. At least a dozen confirmed."

"Are they headed here?" Perhaps Melanie's words weren't an idle threat.

"Yes, they'll be headed towards you," said Siobhan. "Otuo put out a call. I put out a call as well that Melanie's there and I can put out another one that Otuo's dead but—"

"Time is limited," I said.

As soon as more fallen showed up, I was done for.

"Not to insult you, old friend," said Siobhan, "but you aren't equipped to fight them. You're—"

"Too pale skinned," I said, "and I sneak around by walking down the middle of the street. I know."

"You're good with vampires," she offered.

I wasn't as good as she was. All the same, I appreciated the compliment. "I'll just concentrate on living long enough for you to teach me how to kill fallen," I said. "Melanie's got Liana, though."

"Oh… is she alive?"

I explained Liana's ploy and her theory that Gamlat was now a resident of the demon realm.

Siobhan let out a low whistle. "Clever girl."

"She's bought herself twenty minutes."

"Okay… well, we can't head to your position right now. I wish we could—"

"But you have to worry about saving the world."

"And we're over an hour away. Also, the Citadel may be in danger. There are unconfirmed reports of fires in Istanbul."

Great… I thought. "You fight your battles," I said. "I'll fight this one."

"Be careful. Why do I have the feeling this is the last time I'll ever talk to you?"

"Because we've never beaten odds this long before?" I suggested. "But I'll see you again, in this world or the next."

"Aye. Good luck, my friend."

"And to you." I hung up, put the phone back in the bag, and surveyed my options. Cassie had to be somewhere nearby; I doubted that Melanie would be wasteful enough to kill or dispose of her. The problem was that Liana was being tested and would be dead or turned in twenty minutes. I couldn't look for Cassie, couldn't even pause very long to plot strategy. I focused on the RV.

Twenty minutes, I thought. *Can I break in in twenty minutes?*

THIRTY-THREE

There were some tall trees near enough to the RV that, after stashing the convenience store bag under a rock, I was able to shimmy up and leap from their branches onto the roof. I landed as lightly as possible, grateful that the vehicle had enough armor to dampen any impact.

The door was tricky to open. I had to lie down on the unyielding metal and slide my upper body off the edge, my balance precarious, the edge of the roof digging hard into my stomach. My arm wasn't long enough to reach the handle, but I was able to strip my shirt off and wrap it around the blade of my dagger. Hooking the edge of the hilt under the latch allowed me to lift it with one convulsive yank, and the door swung inward as I tumbled back onto the roof.

There came a shout of alarm from inside the RV. My veil hadn't been strong enough to make whoever was in the way of the door move aside. This was a problem sometimes when the object I moved was too far away from my body, and when my adversary was on guard and more likely to resist the urge to step aside.

It wouldn't take long for them to figure out that I was on the roof. I had to move. I peered down through the door to get an idea of what and who were where. There was enough empty space behind the door guard that I could make a safe landing inside. I pulled my shirt back on and sheathed my dagger.

This next step was a challenge. I leaned backwards over the edge of the roof until I could grip the top of the door frame. With as much control as I could manage, I brought my knees to my chest and somersaulted off, my body still curled up as I swung myself down and through the doorway. Because I'd vaulted backwards, I was able to see into the RV as I swung in, and that allowed me to launch myself over the head of the human waiting to stab me and land in the middle of the room, away from the cluster of vamps at the back. I clipped the door guard behind the ear with my foot, though, and that meant he saw me.

I spun to face the vamps first, since they moved faster, even though the human was closer. My dagger was in my hand. A block with one of my wrist cuffs, then one thrust, two, and they were dust. I rounded on the human and stabbed his chest before he knew what hit him. I ducked away from the touch of a third vampire and stabbed him to dust as well.

I didn't like killing people, even if they allied with vampires. They were still humans and children of God. Nevertheless, this was precisely the kind of situation that required it, the loophole that Otuo tried to invoke to kill Liana and her friends.

A flash out of the corner of my eye was Melanie zipping out the door. She had me trapped, so she was going to see if her minions could finish me off before putting herself at risk.

Well, I hadn't fought for two thousand years without gaining some skills, and here, in close quarters with the element of surprise on my side, I was able to dispatch the fourth and last vamp with a feint, a spin, and a thrust.

Liana watched, eyes wide.

"Better than the girl's bathroom?" I asked as I slammed and locked the door of the RV.

Melanie's fuming voice came over a speaker system. "Did any of them survive? Fools! I told them he was tricky."

I found the little monitor that showed the cluster of vampires and humans near the door, Melanie scolding them with so much venom that I wondered that none of them poofed to dust from her gaze alone.

"Get this door open! Who has the key!" she shouted.

"They're inside, Madam."

"I know they're inside," she bellowed.

"I mean the keys…"

Liana snorted with laughter.

"That'll slow them down," I said. "It won't stop them."

"I know." Liana rubbed her face with the cloth of her shirt, doing her best to clear away the dust and grime.

"They'll pull out Cassie next," I said. "Threaten to torture her unless we open the door."

"Yeah they can try." Liana's smile was knowing. "The thing is, when they were trying to move her, she got loose and ran into a nail salon to get some nail clippers."

"To cut her toenails?" I asked. That was a running joke between us, that cutting toenails was one way to activate the standing spell to shield a home.

Liana's smile indicated it wasn't a joke after all. "None of the vamps could get into the salon. How much you wanna bet the place offered pedicures?"

"Well they've got humans working with them," I said. "They'll go get Cassie."

Liana's face fell. She looked around the inside of the RV. "While they're trying to retake this vehicle, you have them at a bottleneck. They'll come through the door one at a time and you can pick them off."

"Melanie—"

"Isn't stupid. I know." Liana leaned against the wall. "I'm the stupid one."

"You're not," I said.

"It was my idea to come out here. We should have gone with Siobhan and Mouse. I played right into Melanie's hands."

"Because you're a good person," I said. "What else are you supposed to do when someone you love is being held captive?"

"Doing the right thing may save a person eternally, but in this moment, are you seriously going to say we aren't doomed mortally?" She shrugged.

"Hey," I said. "We totally have a chance of winning this. Maybe if it takes them long enough to get that outer door open, they'll even forget we're here and we'll have the element of surprise all over again."

As she had before, even in the most dire situations, Liana laughed.

And I joined her. What else were we to do? I laughed until my sides would have ached. Then my gaze fell on the blackout area. "Well, actually," I said, going over to trace my fingers over the lock and open the door. "You get in here. It'll give you an extra layer of protection. Hide in here and clip your toenails."

Liana came to peer in. "This... if I didn't know who owned this RV, I'd think it was some kind of rape van."

There was no reason to point out that it might be. Vampires did whatever they wanted, regardless of who got hurt. "Just get in there."

A sudden bang from the direction of the door made us both jump. I checked the monitors and saw that a few vampires were ramming the door with what looked like a downed street light. In that battle, the door would eventually lose.

Liana still hadn't moved. "Your reflexes," she said, "they aren't supernatural right? You just got them that fast by training?"

"Right. My kind don't get the super speed that vampires do. Don't ask me why."

Liana bit her lip, then looked at me. "All of Melanie's tracking equipment is in here? Inside this RV? Her infrared sensors and stuff to find me?"

"Yeah," I said. "I think so."

Another crash.

"Then…" Liana stepped towards me. "Maybe we *can* have the element of surprise?" The color had drained from her face. Her throat convulsed as she swallowed, hard. One more step closer and she pressed her palm against my chest. The heat from her body suffusing into me.

I looked down at her ragged nails and roughed up skin.

Never had my lack of heartbeat created such a void in my chest. *What are you doing?* I wanted to ask her, but I feared that if I did, I wouldn't like the answer, that I'd find out she was just trying anything and everything to forestall our deaths.

She pulled back, removed the rings from her fingers and put them in her pocket, then laid her palm on my chest again. I didn't breathe as she slid her hand up until her fingers reached the bare skin at the nape of my neck.

THIRTY-FOUR

P ain exploded down my spine when her fingers made contact with my skin, and I gasped, causing her to rear back.

"Sorry," she whispered.

"No, it's okay. Liana…" I didn't know if I meant that as a plea or protest, but I didn't move or resist as she stepped up, backing me against the wall of the blackout area, the heat of her body enveloping me.

All of those thoughts and dreams from my year as a mortal came flooding back. I put my arms around her waist, pressing her closer as her breath tickled across the skin of my neck.

She pushed a lock of my hair back from my face, sparks of pain ignited as her fingertips brushed my forehead. Then she leaned up, her breath hot against my lips. Her kiss was gentle, hesitant, and the sting was sharp, but not unbearable. When she broke it off, I leaned after her and kissed her back, more firmly, letting the agony burn through me.

This, I told myself, was like sunrise was for her. This was burning the demonic taint out of my body. As this thought took hold, I pulled her more firmly against me, pain exploding across my senses.

We were both breathing hard now, and when we broke off the kiss, the sharp sting of her touch didn't fade. Whatever process had started would continue now. There was no stopping it. Kissing her again would only speed it up. Reality was a haze as the pain scorched hotter, but still I leaned in, only to feel her pull back.

"Is this okay?" Her hand cupped my cheek, causing a duller pain that I didn't even flinch at.

I gazed down at her, those brown eyes filling my universe. "Yeah," I whispered between gasps. "It's more than okay."

"Am I hurting you?"

"I don't want you to stop, if that's what you're asking."

"Corban—"

"Please," I begged her. "Unless you don't want—"

She silenced me with another kiss, one that wasn't hesitant at all.

More pain shot through me and I found myself gripping the back of her shirt in my clenched fists while her hands stroked down my chest.

That was too intense and it was my turn to pull back, only she didn't stop kissing me. Instead she moved to make a trail of kisses down the side of my neck, which also burned, but at this point the pain was starting to shift.

A sensation like a hard punch against the inside of my sternum made my vision swim. I leaned back against the wall as another punch came, then another. When Liana paused, her breath tickling my collarbone, I cupped her jaw in my hand and leaned forward to kiss her on the lips again. This time it barely hurt at all.

My heart felt like it was thrashing and spasming in my chest as a sensation like acid spread through my body, burning away my powers and immortality as it went. Liana now felt warm against me, rather than burning hot. She paused, feeling my warm breath against her skin, no doubt.

My chest ached as my heart strained, overworking itself after spending so much time dormant.

"You okay?" Liana whispered. Her hand against my cheek was all comfort now, no pain.

"Yeah," I whispered, turning to kiss her palm.

Another bang on the door startled us both.

"Well, good," she said. "Because I think they're just about inside."

Liana retreated from me, taking all her warmth and comfort with her.

With a few wheezing breaths, I managed to get my vision clear. I was exhausted, on the brink of collapse, but I didn't have time for that right now.

Another bang sounded from outside and I felt the shockwave through the floor. I took a step, stumbled, and fell into Liana's arms.

"I'm okay," I assured her, pressing my lips to her forehead as if it was the most natural thing in the world. To prove my point, I flicked my dagger into my hand, then slipped it back in its sheath. "You get in there." I pointed to the blackout area.

Liana ducked in, the door clicking shut behind her.

She was safe.

The screens mounted on the wall showed Melanie and company standing outside the door, firing up a blowtorch. Their pounding on the door had dented it and opened up the seam between the door and its frame. A timer in the bottom corner of the screen said how long they had until sunrise—hours, still. It wasn't coming fast enough to save me.

The keys that Melanie wanted so desperately were on the floor, on a keychain with a little fluffy cat on it. I picked them up and stuffed them in my pocket.

I had to assume Melanie had dispatched some of her goons to go get Cassie. My goal was to kill as many of Melanie's followers as I could as fast as I could. Killing Melanie was unlikely; she'd no doubt retreat and wait for Cassie to be brought to her, or just retreat off into the woods and disappear for now.

I stretched, feeling my muscles and bones pop in an alien, meaty way. A few bounces on the balls of my feet, a hard shake to loosen my shoulders, and I was ready for action. Time to take command of the situation.

With one hand I drew my dagger, and with the other I flung open the door. The vampire on the other side hadn't been expecting that. I knifed him and fell back before the others even registered what had happened. The blowtorch dropped to the ground, setting alight the debris that littered the asphalt. Flames leapt up, creating a blast of heat that I had to back away from.

"Get in there!" Melanie shouted.

There wasn't enough dry fuel on the ground for the flames to last long, so it wasn't going to be much of an advantage.

A human leapt across the flames. He didn't come at me and I shifted aside to watch as he headed for the control panel.

That wasn't the direction I expected him to go, since the keys had been elsewhere, but before he could do whatever it was he was going to do, I was on him. A stab in the heart and he went down, blood pouring out of the wound. That was going to make fighting in here extra treacherous.

The control panel he'd lunged for wasn't clearly marked. Hardly a surprise. Melanie knew how to layer on the security and ensure that even if this control center fell into enemy hands, such enemy wouldn't know what was what.

Context gave me some clues, though. Melanie wanted her keys, or more precisely, she wanted control over this vehicle. Perhaps this panel included switches that would enable her to control the RV from her cellphone?

I jammed my dagger into the panel and was rewarded with a massive spark of electricity that made me leap back.

My dagger was stuck, probably still channelling that electricity. Quickly, I pulled out the dagger Mouse had left for me and gazed with regret at the one I'd lost.

"Flood it!" came a shouted order from outside.

Smoke came billowing into the RV. It wasn't from the fire; that had burned itself out. That meant it wasn't smoke at all, it was mist, or more specifically, vampires in mist form.

If I was still ascended, I would have been burned to a crisp the moment the mist came in contact with my body, but as I was now, it wouldn't affect me. That didn't mean it couldn't be deadly, though. There was Liana's trick of sending tendrils of mist into my nose and making my lungs explode. Besides that, I didn't want to give away just yet that I was human now.

I vaulted out of the RV and slammed the door shut behind me, stabbing two vampires who were standing too close before I landed in the parking lot.

In a flurry of strikes and blocks with my wrist cuffs, I took out four more vampires and another human.

I had to find Melanie. If I was to take her out, I had to rush her before Cassie could be brought into the situation, and before Melanie figured out I wasn't ascended.

Yipping howls sounded in the distance.

Probably just regular coyotes, I thought. Nevertheless, all of Melanie's minions scattered at the sound, which surprised me. Then again, it might not have been the sound, but the fact that their mistress wasn't here to order them to fight.

Where was Melanie?

With a flourish, she stepped out from behind one of the SUVs, dragging Cassie by her hair. Liana's aunt did her best to keep up, but her captor yanked relentlessly and Cassie's face was stained with tears. Her feet were bare and bloody and her dress ripped.

Two human bodies still lay on the ground at my feet. For a few seconds, and no more, Melanie might be fooled into thinking that the smell of humanity that emanated from me was actually emanating from them.

That gave me very little time to act. I bolted for Melanie, letting myself stumble just as I had when trying to take out Darissa in the girls bathroom at Taos High.

Just like her sister, Melanie took the bait. Like a shot, she let go of Cassie and came at me, knocking me over backwards onto the pavement, my head hitting hard enough that I saw stars. Melanie knelt on my chest, her hands around my throat. It was the move that Darissa had nearly killed me with. Melanie's eyes widened as she realized my skin was warm, not cold. That didn't throw her off balance for long, though. All she had to do was squeeze to hurt me, and squeeze she did.

But since she had begun this attack as if she was taking down an angel, she hadn't pinned my arms. As the world grayed out, I brought my dagger up and plunged it into her back. She gasped but didn't let go, and didn't disintegrate. I'd missed her heart.

Ferrum, however, was still poison to her. Rather than stab again, I twisted the dagger, grateful for its wider blade, then yanked the hilt to one side.

The only problem was that my world was going dark and my grip wouldn't hold. I felt my fingers release.

She'd cut off my oxygen supply.

I was suffocating.

And then her hands disintegrated and I was able to breathe. My first breath, though, was chock full of dust, which I coughed up so violently the muscles of my ribcage felt like they were being ripped free.

"Corban." Cassie's voice.

I could see her silhouette standing over me, the blowtorch in her hands. She fumbled with it, trying to turn it off, then gave up and threw it aside. "What the hell was that?" she shouted.

Another yipping howl cut across the predawn, joined by another, then another. Lithe canine figures burst from the wreckage of the town and converged on the RV and cars. Headlights shone up the street, followed a moment later by a minivan which stopped with a screech of tires on asphalt.

"Corban? Liana?" Siobhan's voice was desperate, terrified.

"You are too late!" Cassie shouted back. "Where were you fifteen minutes ago?" She spun around. "How weird is this going to get, Corban?"

"Very," I said. "And I'm sorry."

The coyotes were all shifting, their canine bodies elongating into human forms. It was the sort of event that none of my kind had ever seen before. Very few beings of any kind would have seen it before.

"There are a couple of vampires in the RV that'll have Liana trapped," I called out to Siobhan. "Someone please get Cassie out of here? Anyone able to convince her this was all a dream?"

THIRTY-FIVE

"You left a tamer of demons alone with a fallen tamer of demons and one of the most powerful vampires in history!" a purple haired woman was shouting at Siobhan.

Siobhan hadn't had a chance to clean up, so her skin was still streaked with grime and her hair was knotted and snarled.

I watched them through a small window in the door—they were in a conference room, standing in front of a chalkboard, upon which was drawn a complex diagram that I gathered was a breakdown of the different realms, with the demon realm marked with a giant X.

It was confusing. Everything that had happened since we'd defeated Melanie was confusing. We'd gotten Liana out of the RV in the Ski Valley and tried to get Cassie a ride back to Taos, but that proved too dangerous. Roberto Morales fell with a loud crack of thunder while we were still figuring out which keys started which vehicles and when I streamed the news on my phone, there was a montage of fires and tidal waves and other extreme disasters that made the fall of Rome look like a minor blip.

"You can stay with us," I told her. "But you may not want to. We can fly you somewhere to safety."

Quirky as she was, she'd kept a straight face when she said, "I'm mentally ill, not crazy. I'm staying with you guys while whatever's happening happens. Can you please try not to be too weird, though?" She took one look at the nearest coyote, a guy whose hair grew in brown and blond zebra stripes, and flashed him a smile. He smiled back and by the time I'd managed to start the first SUV, those two were talking.

I'd passed out at some point after we got that first SUV running and awoke in the back of the sedan, which was cruising across an endless desert with Aline at the wheel and Liana in the passenger seat. I had the back seat to myself.

"Where are we?" I'd asked.

"Does this look like anywhere?" Aline had snapped at me, as if my question was stupid. Liana shot me a helpless look of confusion.

We'd driven for what felt like hours with the SUVs and RV following us. I drifted in and out of wakefulness, and the landscape never changed until we came upon what appeared to be an abandoned hospital. It stood alone on the flat, lifeless plain, yet had electricity and running water. The signs were all written in a language I'd never seen, the letters an odd set of squiggles vaguely reminiscent of Arabic.

I'd had a chance to shower and brush my teeth and change into clean clothes—Aline had retrieved our bags from the rental car. One thing about being human again was getting used to how my body reeked. I had to resist the urge to shower for hours, especially out in this strange, remote place where it didn't seem possible to buy any deodorant, and there wasn't any in the bag of convenience store food and such—which one of the coyotes had located while searching the Ski Valley.

As I was toweling off, I could sense more people arriving. Gone was my ability to taste emotions; the world was blessedly quiet in that respect, but the distant sounds of voices and footsteps telegraphed to the bathroom where I combed out my hair and wondered where Liana was. She'd been ushered to a different room when we arrived.

By the time I emerged, all cleaned up, the building was quiet again. I wandered the darkened hallways until I found a beacon of light shining through the small window in a door that, upon closer inspection, proved to lead to the conference room, where the purple-haired coyote-woman chewed Siobhan out for leaving me and Liana to fight Otuo and Melanie alone.

Siobhan wasn't having it. Her eyes flashed murderously from her grimy face framed by frazzled hair. "Angels are falling all over the place," she said. "The Citadel has fallen. We've been distracted!"

"Your kind were responsible for the demon realm," said the purple-haired woman. "That was your number one responsibility. You start seeing something different with vampires, you should have looked into it. And how could you have forgotten that

Gamlat was the first vampire? Otuo's wife who tried to expel her demon and instead became untouchable to him?"

"We had vampires tearing up our records nonstop," said Siobhan. "As for Liana—"

"Look, if I may," said a female voice belonging to someone I could not see from my vantage point, "My kind sent me to live with Liana in college for all four years, because it was *obvious* she was a tamer of demons. How stupid are you guys?"

"The Sidhe should also have seen the next opportunity to contain the demon realm," The purple-haired woman had her back to me; I had yet to see her face. "You've worked with the angelic order before."

"Yeah, before Otuo started going a little nuts, sure," said Liana's Sidhe roommate. "Besides, I was living with Liana for four years and nobody contacted me. What else were we supposed to do? It's not like we can just call up the angelic order, you know? You're *invisible.*"

"You lot," Siobhan shouted back at the purple haired woman, "shouldn't have been skulking around in the shadows all this time. You lot were the ones who really knew what to look for, and it's bloody impossible to find you unless you want to be found, which is *never.*"

"I have to agree," said the roommate. "If the realms were so far out of balance, why weren't the coyote-shifters looking for the next tamer of demons?"

A soft footstep behind me made me turn. Liana stood in the middle of the hallway, her hair wet and smelling like conditioner, her skin clean and her body garbed in a loose sweatshirt and leggings that I averted my gaze from. Her eyes were wide and questioning. "What are they talking about?"

"I can't say for sure, but something to do with your life becoming a lot more complicated from now on."

"Oh, right. Where's Cassie?"

I shrugged. "No idea. I just hope she's doing okay. I thought I knew how weird the universe was. Turns out all I saw was the tip of the iceberg."

"Well," she said, looking past me into the conference room, "I figured out where we are, kind of. One of the coyotes I met in the hallway said that this isn't Earth, but it isn't another realm either. It's a kind of nether space where they sometimes bring people who have to flee their own realms but can't go to Earth or vice versa."

"Oh, well that clears things up," I said.

"Doesn't it though?" She laughed, but it was a short bark of a laugh. She wasn't in a mirthful mood. Her gaze had turned instead to me once more. "Um…" she began.

I waited for her to say more, even though I dreaded whatever it would be. She bit her lip and looked down.

Which meant it was my job to be the grown up. "Look," I said. "You don't owe me anything, all right?"

Her gaze, when she lifted it again, was unreadable.

"I know you've been working hard to get over me," I said. "And I appreciate you saving our lives back there, but it doesn't have to mean anything."

Her eyes widened and her chin began to tremble. "But…" she whispered.

In a flash I had my arms around her, hugging her close, her warm body against my chest. "Or it can mean something," I whispered in her ear.

She relaxed and snuggled in closer.

"Ahem."

We both froze. I let go of Liana and we both turned to face Siobhan.

My old friend stood in the hallway with her feet planted and her arms folded. The door to the conference room was swinging shut behind her. "Sorry to interrupt."

"Look," I began. "The thing is—"

"I don't care," Siobhan cut me off. "Really, I don't. I'm too tired to care. Here's the deal, a lot of angels have fallen and more keep falling on Earth and it's going to be a mess. A full blown supernatural war. You—" she pointed at Liana "—need to work with the Sidhe and the coyotes to stop it. And you—" she pointed at me "—um… I'm guessing you're going to do what you want."

"If she's going into danger, I go too," I said.

More people were filing out of the conference room. The purple-haired woman, Liana's former roommate (who now looked middle aged), Amy, Gina, Cassie, and Aline along with several other coyotes filled the hallway.

I looked over at Liana. She squared her shoulders.

"So," said Aline. "Like, we need you to go to the demon realm and, like, fix the problem of demons invading Earth. We failed last time we had a tamer of demons. Looks like we get another chance."

Liana looked sidelong at me. "I guess I don't need to worry about grad school applications, then?"

ACKNOWLEDGMENTS

I need to thank my first and most loyal beta reader, Char Peery (yes, we still call each other by our maiden names. That's how long we've known each other.) Thanks also to my ARC readers, for catching other typos and proofing errors: Pat Johnston, Jeff Ney-Grimm, Viola Braxmaier, and Melodie Kolmetz.

This book was edited by Trent Zelazny, a talented author in his own right, and a friend. You can often find us at a local coffee shop, talking about the ins-and-outs of the publishing industry. A further round of edits and rewrites were guided by Jane Lindskold (author of the *Firekeeper* novels among other iconic works of fantasy. My personal favorite is *Child of a Rainless Year*, if you're looking for a great read.)

Formatting was done by E.M. Tippetts Book Designs (emtippettsbookdesigns.com), specifically Stacey Millett Tippetts (ebook) and Tara Jones (paperback)—with Tianne Samson rounding out the team. The cover layout was a collaboration between me and Linda Caldwell, our in-house cover designer. Everything beautiful about these books is thanks to them.

And as always, thank you to my family, who have tolerated me putting myself through a punishing schedule to get all three of these books out within six months. I hope they still remember what I look like when this is all done!